THE GRID 2

QUEST FOR VENGEANCE

PAUL TEAGUE

ALSO BY PAUL TEAGUE

Sci-Fi Starter Book - Phase 6

The Secret Bunker Trilogy

Book 1 - Darkness Falls

Books 2 - The Four Quadrants

Books 3 - Regeneration

With Jon Evans

Book 1 - Incursion

Book 2 - Armada

Book 3 - Devastation

CHAPTER ONE

Inferno

Joe had no time to grieve for Zach. The flames were roaring around them. They were throwing out heat like he'd never experienced before. The crackling, searing blaze encircled them, intimidating the twelve captives and creating instant panic and terror. Zach was dead, he could see that. There was nothing he could do. The rage surged in him once again, but now was not the time for anger.

Joe looked to Clay who was taking a lead. They'd need Clay to help them survive – his instincts were good. Lucy was trying to comfort the man from the Institute. He was screaming now. Joe had never seen a raw terror like that. He tried to assess the situation, it had happened so fast. One minute they'd been looking out into some dark hangar, and the next the flames rose from nowhere and their environment had completely changed.

'Look for clues,' Joe told himself. He'd never taken much notice of The Grid trials, they turned his stomach to watch. However, he knew the format well enough. They would not all be killed at once – the purpose was to prolong these events. Fortrillium wanted the full attention of The City. It wouldn't want to finish the trial straight away, which meant there was a solution to this – there was always a way out. Until the very last person was left standing, there was always a way out.

Joe scanned the area. They were in a wooded terrain – it was incredible how the environment had changed around them, but the heat from the flames was real enough. He was wet with sweat, and his face felt as if it was burning already. There seemed to be nothing there to help them, but there had to be a way out, there was no way Fortrillium would allow them all to perish in the opening minutes of the trial. Joe looked around desperately. There was no water, nothing with which to protect themselves, he just couldn't see a solution.

They were in a clearing, encircled by trees, with the fire surrounding them. Zach's burned body was at his feet. He'd been forced to run from inside the fire, he didn't stand a chance.

Clay seized the initiative. He'd been doing the same as Joe, but found a solution faster. He shouted over the cries of the other prisoners. Only one of them seemed unmoved by the terror of the situation. It was the man in the black overalls, the killer. He just stood in the dead centre of the group, smiling. It was as if he were challenging death to a duel, he seemed to have no fear.

'We need to stay calm!' Clay shouted above the noise. 'We can survive this, but we have to pull together. We're not going to burn here, but we've got to protect ourselves from the heat.'

Clay moved to the centre of the clearing, right next to the man in the black overalls, and picked up a nearby stick.

'Create a shallow channel in the dirt – we need to pull the earth over us to protect us from the heat. Make sure you cover as much of your skin as possible. Pull your sleeves down if you have them rolled up. The fire can't get us, but the heat and the smoke can.'

Everybody followed Clay's lead, and Joe moved towards Lucy to help with the man in yellow overalls.

'He's called Chris,' Lucy shouted over the sound of the blaze.

'Chris, help us to dig,' Joe said as calmly as he could. Chris was good, he had no problem following the others, and he was less agitated with something to do.

Clay moved fast. He had his trench created first. The flames were getting nearer. The fugitives were coughing, gasping for breath, as they frantically created shallow channels in which to seek sanctuary. Clay was clearing the surrounding area of sticks and debris in an attempt to create a safe zone.

'Cover your mouths and keep low!' he shouted.

'The flames can't reach us, it's the heat that'll kill you.'

Lucy and Joe helped Chris into his trench and pushed the dirt over him as best they could.

'We'll be right next to you all the time,' Lucy said. 'Try to stay calm.'

On a screen in The Climbs, Chris's parents looked at the terrible scene playing out before them. They whispered a prayer, thanking whoever it was who was protecting their son in The Grid. On the screens they were calling him Rampage, his humanity didn't matter in there. The girl and her friend were looking out for him, and if there was any way they could repay them, they would. The girl calmed him, as his mother had done before he'd been forcibly removed to the Institute. She knew he wasn't violent – he just needed to be soothed. That's exactly what she saw the girl doing on the screen.

With Chris now placid and still, Lucy and Joe joined the others lying face down in their hastily dug trenches, doing their best to pull soil over themselves. Clay was the last in the ground. He was coughing badly as he kicked the last of the soil over Joe's back, his red and sore eyes squinting from the intense smoke.

The flames were as close as they were going to get now. There were twelve of them lying still in the centre of the dirt circle coughing furiously and waiting for the flames to pass.

Joe could feel the thin layer of dirt covering his back become warm, but it was not burning him. He was so hot and desperate for water. His body was dripping with sweat.

Fortrillium would not finish them there and then, he was sure of that. There was usually a way to survive, but you had to spot it. He thanked his good fortune for having Clay in their group. The others had been useless, nobody knew what to do. Joe didn't know what to do either. He'd been too slow to see the solution. He'd have to sharpen up if they were going to survive this.

He pulled the collar of his overalls further over his mouth, closed his eyes tight, and like the other eleven Justice Seekers prayed that the shallow trench would not become his grave.

Force

Talya had not wanted to hurt Max Penner, but he was clearly more scared of Fortrillium than he was of her. She understood his fear. As she'd prepared to kick down his door, she was terrified – not just for her own life, but for everything that she was about to do. It was the realization that she was committed to a course of events and there was no way out now.

The exits had been sealed the minute she became a Law Lord. Damien Hunter had forced the issue when he arrested Lucy. It would either end in Hunter's death or her own. One of them would not escape this scenario.

If only Talya hadn't got Lucy to think about. If she could act on her own, it would be better. But everything she did, she had to consider Lucy. It was knowing that the trial was about to begin that had urged her to violence. She knew Max was hiding something. There was no time to dance around the issue.

He certainly hadn't been expecting her to burst through his door after their encounter in the street. She felt ashamed of herself, but she'd seen the fear in his eyes when she stormed up to him in his house. Like a bully, she could smell fear on her victim and she knew he was vulnerable.

'Tell me what that was on your desk, Mr Penner. I won't ask you again!'

'Get out of my house. You have no right to burst in here, I'll tell Fortrillium, they'll never allow it—'

Talya wasn't playing that game anymore. She'd spotted a carving knife on the worktop next to where Max was standing, his left hand resting on the kitchen table. He'd been preparing a meal. She picked up the weapon and plunged it into the centre of his hand, bones cracking and splintering as it tore through his flesh. Max screamed. She winced – she'd never had to use violence before, but she had to get Max to talk.

'Tell me about the WristCom!'

Max was crying, desperate to get the blade out of his

hand, but it had lodged securely into the wooden table as it passed through his flesh.

'I can't tell you anything. You know they'll kill me!'

'I'll kill you if you don't talk. My daughter is in The Grid, and I'm not going to let her die if there's a way to save her.'

Talya took the handle of the knife and rocked it from side to side. She heard Max's flesh tearing. She wanted to be sick. She hated herself for what she was doing. Max was a victim like everyone else. If the sacrifices they were making were going to be worthwhile, there would be more deaths, more suffering to come. Talya had to make it matter – she deserved to perish if she couldn't make what she was doing count for something.

'Max, just tell me!'

'I can't,' he cried through his pain. 'Please, just leave me out of this!'

Talya grabbed his skewered hand and twisted it. The blade tore more flesh. Max screamed out in agony.

'Tell me!'

'It had been hidden in one of the dead bodies – I found it ...'

Max was speaking through tears of pain, his whole face contorted.

'Whose body?'

'The one who got to the end of the last trial – they called him Jay, I think.'

'Where is it now?'

'I don't know. Honest, I don't know!'

'Tell me what happened to it after you took it off your desk.'

'I can't, they'll kill me. I don't want to die in there.'

In spite of the terrible pain, Max would still rather deal with Talya than face Fortrillium and The Grid.

Talya pushed his hand into the direction of the blade, and it cut further into his flesh. He screamed again, writhing to escape from his torturer. The kitchen table was smeared crimson, the floor below sticky with blood.

'I sent it in there. I tried to look inside, alright?'

Talya looked at him and moved towards his hand. Max flinched. Talya despised herself.

'Where is it now?'

'It's still in there. I lost it.'

'Does anybody know about it?'

'No, just me, but I need to get it out of there. If they find it they might trace it back to me.'

'Can you still connect to it?'

Max was silent. He knew he'd never shake her off if he answered.

'Can you still connect to it?'

Still no answer.

Talya grabbed Max's wrist and pushed it towards the blade with all the force that she could muster. It was nearing his fingers now, she'd almost torn right through his hand.

He let out another scream. She felt as if she was going to pass out from the barbarity of what she was doing.

'Yes, yes!'

Max just wanted it to stop now.

'I can still connect to it, but it's lying there on the floor. I can't get to it.'

Talya relaxed. She'd got the information she wanted. She felt woozy from the violence of the past few minutes. She was sickened by the sight of the torn flesh.

Max felt the tension easing, and he looked down at his

hand. His face was white. Talya hadn't noticed that – he was ashen.

She watched his eyes fade as he passed out. Instinctively she rushed to break his fall, but she was too slow. Max fell to the ground, and as he did so she heard the sickening ripping sound of flesh as the knife tore through the rest of his hand.

Talya had finally got the information she'd come for. She cursed Damien Hunter for the things he was forcing her to do, but now she had a way to communicate with Lucy – if they could get the WristCom to her, they might all stand a chance.

She felt dizzy. The sudden ending of the violence had made her exhausted and weak. She vomited painfully, as if her body were rejecting what she'd had to become to torture Max. She understood his fear and she wished him no harm. He was acquiescent, like the rest of them. His only crime was wanting to stay alive.

It was not over for Max. She'd patch him up and apologize to him for what she'd done, but if he wouldn't help her with what was coming next, she'd do it all over again – and worse.

Before she began the next part of her interrogation, she needed to place another request with Damien Hunter in her capacity as Law Lord. If he'd felt inconvenienced by her last visit, he was going to like this one even less.

Death Sentence

Reevil96 watched the live close-up of Zach Fuller's grip loosening as Joe held his hand, offering a final gesture of comfort before he died. The cameras caught everything in The Grid, and they'd zoomed in on that final moment of life. It would be a boost for the engagement scores, a poignant scene like that was good for everybody.

Hannah had done well. He had to try to think of her as Janexx2. That was who he was competing against here; he had to view her as competition, not a human being. She was good, better than the rest. He couldn't figure it out, her style of gameplay was different.

He'd first observed it in the Gridders' challenges. The other players knew the games well – they were masters of gaming conventions. But Hannah stood out. She was obviously comfortable in the gaming environment, but she was more advanced than the rest. It was as if she'd not only studied gameplay, but also human psychology. She was always a step ahead of her opponents. She anticipated the games; she could read her opponents well –her strategic thinking was astonishing. It was as though she'd profiled the Justice Seekers before the gameplay, as if she could read their minds and know what they were going to do before they did.

He would have to watch Janexx2. She was a threat. Her opening to the trial had been magnificent – it was a masterstroke going for a kill so early into the action. Most of the Gridders would have gone for the man from the Institution – Rampage, as he'd become known by the commentators on the screens. It would have been an easy win. She could have tugged at the heartstrings and targeted a Justice Seeker who frankly was never going to be a contender to reach the end of the trial.

But Janexx2 had been cleverer than that. She'd studied the relation dynamics between the Justice Seekers, and she could see that Parsons had a high affinity score with Slater and Fuller, even though none of the Gridders were privy to the names of the Justice Seekers. It was sensible to go for

Fuller – he'd lost a leg, there was only so long he would be able to survive in The Grid anyway.

But to sacrifice him within minutes and disorientate Parsons when under such extreme pressure from the flames? That was pure theatre, it was a perfect moment in The Grid.

It wasn't over yet. Reevil96 was watching the live action on his monitor. He saw views that nobody else got to see. The fire was as close as it was going to get to the Justice Seekers. They were all lying still in their shallow dirt trenches, surrounded by flames.

Janexx2 had played well – this was a great visual scene. The blaze would die soon – they'd be in danger of suffocation or dehydration if it didn't end. This Justice Trial needed to last some time; there was a lot of capital to be gained from having Talya Slater's daughter in there. The one called Clay looked like he was built from the same stuff as Jay. He was going all the way to the end.

He rubbed his eyes and continued to watch the twelve still and silent bodies in their shallow graves. He'd have to watch Janexx2, she was a danger to him. If he let her win, it would be over for him. That's how it worked. Nobody had come even close for many years. But if this Gridder was as good as he thought, he might have to finish her off himself to protect his own family.

CHAPTER TWO

Collaborators

Mitchell had not been subjected to the same inconveniences that President Josh Delman reserved for Damien Hunter. When he'd summoned Mitchell to a meeting, he'd been on time and shown great courtesy.

Mitchell had panicked he'd got the invitation. He'd been making his way back to The Climbs with a bag full of illegal tech. He knew they were after Wiz, but he wasn't sure what his own fugitive status was. Thankfully he'd been away from the sewer on the night the others were caught.

He hoped he'd avoided detection – he was extremely careful with his tech. They couldn't track what he was doing, Mitchell was sure of that. So why had he sensed the black vehicle following him, just as he was about to approach the road to the security gate into The Climbs?

He'd considered running as he watched the car stalking its prey in his peripheral vision. It would be hard to hide in his part of The City, probably impossible. Unlike The Climbs, there were security cameras everywhere. They formed a security matrix throughout Silk Road – there was no hiding in the ruins of the tower blocks as Wiz had been forced to do.

Could he beat the surveillance systems if he went on the run? Mitchell wasn't sure. They'd all got the Gen-ID chips implanted, and they could certainly check which side of The City he was on. But could they locate his whereabouts from that? Mitchell thought not, though they'd be able to get a rough idea of where he was.

A car door opened behind him. Somebody was stepping out of the vehicle. This was his final chance. Should he stay cool or make a run for it? He made the decision in a split second. Whoever was approaching him was alone, there were no Centuria. Her body language was not aggressive. This did not appear to be a detention.

'Mitchell Cranshaw?'

'Yes,' Mitchell replied, still not sure if running was his best option. She was dressed well, very confident and self-assured, extending her hand in welcome. Her arms were uncovered, and Mitchell immediately noticed she had no tattoo. No Gen-ID chip? He'd never seen that before.

He thought back to Wiz. Gestures like a handshake had died out in The Climbs. His friend wouldn't have known how to respond to that approach. They were so different.

Mitchell put out his hand.

'Pleased to meet you.'

'You too,' Mitchell began. She could see that he needed to be reassured.

'I'm Teanna Schaelles. I'm with the President's office. I manage special projects for Mr Delman. He'd like to speak with you, Mitchell.'

Again Mitchell wondered if he should run for his life. Why would the President's office be interested in him?

Sure, he'd made some impressive breakthroughs at work, but it was nothing that would attract Delman's attention. He squeezed the handle on his bag a little tighter – as if that would protect him from anything if they searched him.

Mitchell felt sure it was connected to the side operation he had going on with Hannah, Lucy and the guys, but this approach was not hostile. Teanna Schaelles seemed friendly and respectful. There were no Centuria to be seen anywhere.

'There's nothing at all to worry about,' she continued, sensing his doubt. 'You've caught the attention of the President and he'd very much like to meet you. He wants to seek your expertise on a technical matter.'

Mitchell thought for a moment. Was a polite refusal even an option? He doubted it.

'No problem, Mx Schaelles.'

'Call me Teanna – please.'

'No problem, Teanna. How about next week sometime?'

Her tone changed suddenly. This is what he'd been waiting for. It was a summons, not an invitation.

'Mr Delman wants to see you this evening, Mitchell.'

There was no 'please', no questioning tone at the end of the sentence. It was a statement, not a request.

That's why, after moving through security and into The Climbs, Mitchell delivered the tech to Wiz, did what he had to do and made sure he was back on Silk Road ready for the pick-up. The rendezvous was with Teanna once again; they'd arranged to meet in the same place they'd chatted earlier. Mitchell thought it would be safer that way.

He'd decided not to say anything to Talya or Wiz. That could wait until he had more detail. This was not a detention, it was a matter of seeking his advice. It was flattering to say the least. He'd keep it to himself and share the information if he needed to. Who knew where it might lead to?

Mitchell contemplated running again. This would be his last chance – if he ever got into that car, he'd be trapped. Once he got caught up in the Presidential offices he wouldn't get out unless they wanted him to. He thought better of it, this had been a friendly approach. He'd attract more attention if he made a fuss.

'May I let my parents know my whereabouts?'

'They know already, Mitchell. They're very honoured that their son has been invited to meet the President.'

The friendly tone was back. Surely this was safe for him? If he was being arrested they'd just have grabbed him and thrown him into the back of a van when they'd met earlier, wouldn't they?

'Okay, no problem. Are we travelling in your car?'

'Yes, please step in, Mitchell. There's a seat for you in the middle.'

No chance to escape if he was sandwiched between two people. He gave a final thought to running, then committed to getting inside the car with Teanna. As he shuffled along the back seat, he pressed up against a well-built man. He was suited and armed. He didn't turn to acknowledge Mitchell, just sat there, staring ahead.

'Don't mind Troy, he doesn't speak much,' Teanna smiled. It was the lamest smile Mitchell had seen in a long time. He reckoned Troy didn't need a lot of words in his line of work. His demeanour said it all.

They sat in silence as they drove to the Presidential offices. Security was tight as they entered the gates, but Mitchell got through without any trouble. Teanna and Troy had probably cleared the way already.

He thanked his good fortune, since as he stepped out of

the car he was searched immediately. If they'd caught him with the tech he'd delivered to Wiz earlier, they might have been a little less welcoming.

Teanna escorted Mitchell into the building. There were iron doors, security cameras everywhere, and Troy looka-likes stationed at every entrance. Not a word was said by Teanna. She clearly had status and respect here – there were no security challenges and no ID cards to be swiped.

Eventually they came to a solid white wooden door, the only wooden door he'd spotted in the building. Teanna opened it up without knocking and showed him to the comfortable seating in front of a massive oak desk nestled in the large window.

There was barely time to look around the room before the President entered via a second door. Mitchell hadn't spotted it straight away. It was concealed in the wall.

'Ah, Mr Cranshaw, welcome. I see you've met Mx Schaelles?'

Mitchell jumped out of his seat and shook the President's outstretched hand. His sleeves were rolled up as if he was in the middle of some work. No tattoo, no Gen-ID chip. It was probably because of his status.

'May I call you Mitchell?'

'Of course,' Mitchell stammered. He wasn't sure how to address the President. Like everybody else, he'd grown up with the President's face on the screens, his voice booming out of the speakers. He seemed smaller in person. He was old too, still sturdy, but older than Mitchell had expected.

Teanna sat down and indicated that Mitchell should do the same. The President took a seat too and began to speak.

'Mitchell, we're aware of what you're doing with your friends.'

Mitchell's heart jumped and his stomach knotted. After

all the friendly reassurances, he hadn't been expecting that. He looked at President Delman. Teanna and Delman let the words hang there. The silence was painful. Mitchell felt compelled to speak – that was the whole point of the silent approach, of course.

'Yes, we've been doing some interesting work on—'

Delman held up his hand.

'Enough!

We want to know about your work in the sewer pipes in The Climbs.'

'Oh,' was all Mitchell could say. He didn't know how to respond. What did they know?

More silence. He was sweating now and his face was red. The President and Teanna were old hands at this, they felt none of Mitchell's discomfort.

'Perhaps you'd like to tell us a little more?' Teanna suggested.

Mitchell could see from their faces that he'd been rumbled.

'We haven't really discovered anything. We just found some old wiring down in the sewers and wondered where it went.'

President Delman studied him, and Mitchell felt his face redden further.

'It was just a bit of fun really, nothing serious.'

He'd decided to play the 'daft teenager' card, but Delman and Teanna could see right through him.

'Let me help you, Mitchell,' the President began. 'Two of your friends were detained today and one of them is on the run, isn't that correct?'

Mitchell wondered if his face could turn any redder, he was burning up.

'Um, yes, I think so.'

'You think so? My sources tell me that Joe Parsons and Lucy Slater were detained this morning and that your friend Shen Li is currently wanted by the Centuria. Isn't that correct?'

Mitchell hesitated as he figured out who Shen Li was.

'You mean Wiz?' he asked, then thought better of it. Had he just dropped Wiz in it? He was pleased to see that he hadn't.

'Yes, Shen Li, also known as Wiz,' replied Teanna. She'd checked it on her WristCom as Mitchell had been speaking. Mitchell was embarrassed to admit to himself that he didn't know Wiz's real name. He'd always been Wiz. Mitchell realized they hadn't mentioned Hannah yet. That was good, he'd keep quiet about Hannah unless they asked.

'We seem to have got ourselves into some trouble,' he offered. He still wasn't sure where this was heading.

'You can say that again!' Delman exclaimed, and then calmed himself. He saw the effect he was having on Mitchell – he was clearly terrified. He adopted a different approach.

'It's unfortunate that Mr Hunter is now dealing with your friends, Mitchell. If you'd come to me with any concerns, I might have been able to keep everything away from Fortrillium's attention. However, you've forced my hand now. He's on to you.'

Mitchell was still trying to read the situation – he couldn't tell if he was being courted or admonished.

'You might not be aware, Mitchell, that Damien Hunter is a thorn in my side. There is no love lost between us.'

Mitchell was getting interested. The focus seemed to be moving in a new direction.

'It's most unfortunate that Mr Hunter has apprehended your friends. I would like very much to have worked with you and your companions. What you have achieved so far is nothing short of remarkable. I wish I'd known what you were capable of.'

Mitchell began to relax; he could feel the redness in his cheeks subsiding.

'I want to make you an offer, Mitchell. I think that, bearing in mind the current peril facing your friends, it will be an attractive one.'

Mitchell noticed Teanna looking at Delman as he spoke. There was collusion here. Teanna knew exactly what was going on, she'd known all along. She must be very senior on the President's staff. This was probably why she got to skip the Gen-ID chip. Mitchell nodded and indicated that the President should continue.

'Your friends are in a very dangerous situation, Mitchell. Joe Parsons and Lucy Slater will almost certainly perish in The Grid.'

Mitchell's stomach knotted again. The thought of Lucy ... the prospect of her actually dying in the Justice Trial, hadn't really sunk in. Delman forced him to recognize the truth of the situation.

'Your friend – Wiz, did you say?'

Mitchell and Teanna nodded.

'Your other friend will most likely be caught before long. The Centuria will track him down soon enough. But here's the nub of it, Mitchell. I can see from your profile that your skills are an integral part of this little operation. It probably wouldn't have happened without you?'

Mitchell wasn't sure how to respond to that, and he just gave a silent nod again. He felt that the President was delivering an address. It didn't feel like a dialogue. He was flattered. He was proud to be hearing those words from somebody so senior. Lucy had never acknowledged his contribution – or Joe and Wiz come to that. It was good to hear the President himself could see how important Mitchell had been.

'I want you to work with me – with us,' he continued, gesturing towards Teanna. 'Mx Schaelles is the most trusted member of my team. Whatever you tell her will come straight back to me, she has my complete confidence.'

Mitchell had already seen enough of their relationship to see that they were very close; they appeared to be completely in tune with each other.

'I want you to continue your work with Shen— Wiz, and Teanna will assist you in concealing his whereabouts. However, you report to us now, is that clear?'

'It is, sir, and thank you for your kind words about my technical abilities. It's good to be appreciated.'

Delman's eyes narrowed. He'd just identified Mitchell's weak spot.

'Of course, it's quite clear that you're the brains behind this. After all, you're the one in the President's office right now, aren't you?'

Distracted from the plight of his friends, Mitchell had allowed himself to be flattered. He was not accustomed to the adeptness of a skilled manipulator such as Delman. He'd fallen directly into the honey trap.

'Well, I really appreciate you saying that, sir. It's great to be acknowledged by somebody of your stature.'

'No problem, Mitchell, no problem at all.'

'So what should I do about Hannah James and Talya Slater, sir? They're part of the team too?'

'Are they really?' Delman replied. He looked at Teanna and smiled.

'Now, that we did not know, Mitchell.'

Regret

Hannah was exhausted by the events of the past half hour, she felt as if she were being split in two by an impossible conflict.

On the one hand she was being celebrated by her Gridder colleagues – the engagement scores had gone to an opening high of 9.3. It was difficult not to get caught up in the cheers and enthusiasm, but she knew the sinister truth that had achieved that result.

None of the Gridders got to see the live action on the screen. Their entire experience was gamified, to take the humanity out of the process, and to force them to focus on the strategic elements. All Hannah and the other Gridders could see on any of the screens were pixel representations of what was really going on in The Grid. These were supplied via a separate feed from the camera drones. Multiple angles were available, but from their point of view this was just another game.

The Grid had been specifically developed this way. The teams of psychologists who helped to create it soon realized that the Gridders were far more effective if emotion was removed from the equation. It was easier to go for a kill if it looked as if you were just eliminating a pixel image on a screen. The Gridders were never supposed to think of them as human.

Neither did the Gridders get to know the names of the Justice Seekers. They received psychological profiles and direct feeds from the devices which had been placed into their brains. However, they did not know names. That would have brought emotional responses back into play.

As Hannah sat at her workstation, she had no knowl-edge that she'd just murdered one of the most important people in Joe's life. There had been a gasp of joy from the Gridders as the burning, pixelated image stumbled across their screens.

'Great gameplay, Janexx2!' they cried, impressed by the shocking scenario she'd hurriedly created to grab the attention of the crowds watching on the screens. But it was still raw for Hannah. She'd had to excuse herself and throw up in the restrooms.

She knew that was a human being she'd killed. She understood this had to be done. If it wasn't her executing Justice Seekers, it would be another Gridder. If Joe, Lucy, Wiz and Mitchell were successful, this could be the end of it. It could be the last time that anybody ever had to watch this barbarity.

But when they'd planned this project, nobody had realized that Hannah would be cut off from outside communication. She was stuck in there with the Gridders until the trial was over. She needed to get a message out to them. She didn't know that two of her friends were represented by the pixels on her screen. Two of the shallow earth mounds concealed Lucy and Joe – her audience-pleasing opening to the trial could have killed two of her best friends.

She hadn't expected it to be that tough. When they'd plotted her infiltration of Fortrillium, they had to second-guess how it would work. With all Gridders sworn to secrecy, they'd had to take a chance on how things would play out if Hannah was successful in being recruited to the elite team.

Hannah had killed a man. She knew he was missing a leg too. She'd seen it on the profile. She hated herself for being able to create such a stunning start to a trial. Her sense for great gameplay had claimed the life of a vulnerable man who couldn't even defend himself. She'd chosen him because he had a high affinity rating to two of the other Justice Seekers, 001Green and 002Green, as they were known to her. In reality those numbers referred to Joe and Lucy, Zach was the man who died. He didn't even get a number, he was nameless in Hannah's scenario, just a walk-on character in a gaming scenario.

97TRaider walked up to Hannah and loudly congratulated her on her early achievement.

'You did great!' he exclaimed for the benefit of everybody else in the room. 'You're a natural!'

Then his voice quietened.

'You've got some vomit on your chin, wipe it off.'

Hannah turned to the side and did as he said.

'Don't show weakness, whatever you do.'

She nodded.

'It takes a while to forget they're human,' he continued, 'but after you make enough kills you get caught up in it and just focus on your objective.'

'I feel nauseous thinking about how I killed that man. I can barely believe I did it.'

'You have to get over it, Janexx2. If you crack up in here, you'll join them in The Grid. On my second month here there was one new guy who couldn't take it. He refused to continue taking any part in the trials. They took him away and we continued running his gameplay environment in The Grid. We only found out afterwards that we'd used his own creations against him – he was killed by his own scenarios. They threw him in The Grid and he perished in there within the day. I'm sorry, Janexx2, there's no other way out of here. You have to get your kills in, then they'll let you leave.'

Hannah thought she was going to vomit again. It's one thing agreeing to a course of action and another thing doing it. She was fearful she wasn't up to the challenge. She might break. How many more Justice Seekers could she kill? When it came to it, would she fight harder for her own life or would she let others survive instead of her?

She cursed that they hadn't anticipated her being cut off like this – they'd been sure that they would somehow be able to communicate during the trials. And there she was, trapped on her own and running blind.

There was nothing else for her to do. She'd have to continue contributing to the trial. It was kill or be killed. Hannah would have to trust that the others could find a way to communicate with her so that somehow they'd be able to bring the slaughter to an end.

She felt weary and drained, but there would be little rest. The fire was subsiding in the first trial scenario now; the Justice Seekers would be given some time to recover before they came under threat again.

She nodded at 97TRaider, acknowledging that she'd carry on and not draw attention to herself. At least she had an ally within the Gridders, somebody to look out for her and guide her. She took a deep breath and braced herself for what was to come. She looked at her screen, eager now to get to grips with the latest data and anticipate where the trial might go next.

There were three deaths indicated. She checked the screen again: surely that wasn't correct? She'd sacrificed the man with the crutches to spare the others. One dramatic death to deflect from the loss of multiple lives, it seemed the best way. But three lives? She'd thought they would all get out alive once they'd figured out how to escape the radiant heat of the fire.

The information was accurate. The first death had been the man with crutches, but there were two more. They'd died in their shallow trenches. Life-sign indicators showed one further death from smoke inhalation, another from heart failure. There were only ten Justice Seekers left to fight for their freedom now.

Communication

Wiz was stiff and aching after his time in the sewer. His clothes were wet where he'd stumbled along the pipe-way. He couldn't afford to indulge himself. He had to stay alert for Centuria. He was seventy flights up Pegasus tower block: five more flights to go and he'd reach the top.

Even though he was cursing Mitchell for his absence, Wiz had to hand it to him – he'd come good with the tech. Wiz had successfully set up a wireless link to hop the data from the sewers to Harry's apartment. Mitchell had even had the good sense to bring some relays so the signal could be boosted as it made its way across The Climbs to his new base.

Wiz had a long night ahead of him. He had two more tower blocks to climb. He'd attach the relays to the roofs: that way he'd be able to preserve as strong a signal as possible. Pegasus block was on the outskirts of The Climbs, it was perfect because it gave him a line of sight with the sewer. It was also very high.

He'd encrypted the data flow which scrambled the two feeds they'd accessed: the link to Fortrillium and whatever it was that lay beyond The City's walls. It was too risky to enter the sewers again. He'd succeeded in disabling the cameras and audio feeds for a while, but he didn't think his nerves or his back could take another trip like that, not on his own.

Once he could set up a base and get access to some

decent sunlight for a solar charge, he'd be able to dig in and see what he could find. He'd recorded and scrambled Delman's conversation and was desperate to get to somewhere safe where he could clean up the audio and have a better listen.

At last he reached the top floor and forced open the door to the roof. From that height he could hear the boom of the screens below. The commentators were in a frenzy of excitement. Wiz scolded himself for not running faster up the flights of stairs – his friends were caught up in that trial, their lives were in danger.

The roof was littered with debris left by those who'd taken sanctuary there. As far as Wiz could tell, there wasn't anybody on the roof with him. He knew enough about life in The Climbs to understand that if anybody were there, they'd make themselves scarce, like a rat scuttling down a drain.

He looked up at the decaying communications masts from a former world. This equipment hadn't been used for at least a hundred years and it was rusting and twisted now. Wiz needed to get his relay as high as he could. There was the remainder of a scaffold frame he'd have to climb to reach the highest aerial. He'd attach it there so the signals could be hopped across The Climbs. Wiz didn't much like exposed heights, but he had no choice in the matter. He placed one of his bags at the base of the scaffold, made sure the other was securely fastened around his shoulders, then started the climb to the top.

He could hear the scaffold creaking as he reached for each bar and pulled himself higher. He didn't weigh much. He was sure that if it could still hold the aerial cluster at the top he'd be fine. He'd pulled himself three levels up the scaffold frame when he noticed that one of the bars had rotted through – it wouldn't take his weight. He cursed, wishing he'd seen that before. He could have saved himself some time if he'd avoided that route.

He'd have to make his way along the secure pole he was standing on, towards the side that faced outwards from the tower block. He baulked for a moment. As he looked down, he was only three scaffold levels up and seventy-five levels above ground after that. It wasn't great for him, but he could deal with it. With his path now blocked, if he wanted to head upwards he'd have to navigate around the frame.

Wiz took a moment to breathe and compose himself. He cursed Mitchell again, then checked himself when he thought about Joe and Lucy – they were all that really mattered.

Step by step he worked along the frame to the corner. He held on tightly and looked down. He felt himself sway – it was a long way up, he could barely make out anything below. Nervously, he inched around the corner of the frame. It was a sheer drop, and he clutched tighter and steadied himself on the bar.

It was windy up there. His hair was blowing in his eyes and it was difficult to look up to check his route. Wiz pulled himself up to the fourth level of the scaffolding frame, then the fifth. Each time he had to release his grasp of one pole to pull himself up to the next. The only thing keeping him from a fall of over 320 metres was the grasp of a single hand.

One more level to go. He was beginning to feel light-headed. If he focused on the task, he could keep his mind off the height. Wiz steadied himself once again, then prepared to thrust his right arm upwards to grab the final pole. Once he reached the top level of the scaffold, he'd have access to the aerial and would be able to attach one of the relays in his bag.

He concentrated, tightened the grip of his left hand, then released the grasp of his right. As his right hand found the upper pole and he moved his left hand to join it, he heard a worrying creak. Before he had time to bring his right hand back to the secure pole beneath him, the upper shaft broke free from its rusting bracket and swung outwards.

Wiz let out a cry of panic as the pole swivelled around forty-five degrees, leaving him hanging in the gap between two tower blocks, high above the ground. He was just dangling there, a bag on his shoulders, both hands gripped around a scaffold pole, anchored to the entire frame by a single bracket. Wiz tried to stay calm. He was terrified. His palms were sweaty from the stress, and he could feel them beginning to slip on the pole. One at a time he unclasped each hand, then attempted to re-establish his grip.

His only choice was to make his way back along the pole to the corner of the scaffold. Although the post looked to be securely held in the bracket, there was a lot of play in it. Every time he inched along the pole, it swung, forcing him to wait until it steadied.

Wiz's arms were beginning to tire. He was supporting his full body weight – they felt as if they were being wrenched out of their sockets. He heard another creak of metal and looked towards the bracket. He wasn't sure how long the bolts would hold under such stress.

He was so near the tethered end of the pole, close enough to throw one of his arms towards the secure scaffold frame and hoist himself over. He was scared to put that final strain on the bracket and force himself forward, but Wiz knew it was the only thing he could do. He removed his right hand from the pole and thrust it forward towards the secure rod to his side. As he did so, the end of one of the bolts sheared off, releasing the post from the bracket. Wiz started to fall before his hand could find sanctuary.

He dropped like a dead weight. He knew it was over. Death would surely follow. How long would it take? From that height, it would be just an instant before he hit the ground. He'd seen the bodies of jumpers before, it wasn't pretty. He'd barely had time to register what was happening when he felt a jolt and heard a voice.

'Reach up!'

Wiz was disoriented, he wasn't dropping anymore.

'Reach up, quickly, your bag won't take your weight much longer!'

Wiz looked towards the voice. A hand was being thrust in his direction. He reached out and felt his weight taken by a man who was much stronger than him. He'd grabbed the strap on Wiz's bag as he was falling, and was now helping him back to the side of the tower block roof.

Wiz was so relieved when his body weight finally came to rest on the roof once again that he had to steady himself to make sure it was real.

'Jeez, thank you so much!'

He checked his bag. It was still there, even though the fabric had torn in the rescue. He reached out to his side to steady himself, then looked towards his rescuer.

Wiz cursed himself once again for letting his guard down. He should have taken more care to see whose hand was being offered to assist him. He was standing in front of three Centuria, and they were all heavily armed.

CHAPTER THREE

Joe began to stir. He'd found a strange calm in the dirt trench. After the violent death of Zach and the terror of the flames, it had given him a welcome sense of peace to be face down and alone with his thoughts. He'd heard the crackling of the flames as they ripped through the woodland around them, but he'd immediately seen the sense of Clay's strategy.

They were in no danger from the flames, even though they were surrounded by them. Until the final stages there was always a way out of The Grid trials. Joe had just been slow to see it. Clay was fast to respond. He'd already saved Lucy's life when the jumper had thrown her out of the cage in The Soak. He'd have to follow Clay's lead if they were going to live. He needed to be sharp and look for the solutions. Most Justice Seekers were intimidated by the challenges, and only Clay had shown the steadiness of mind required. And Lucy too, she'd taken care of Chris, she probably saved his life by calming him. He'd been all but ready to run into the flames in his panic.

Joe shook the dirt off his back and turned around in his pit. The flames had stopped, the heat was gone. He had to remember this was an artificial environment, it wasn't real. It certainly felt as if it was authentic, but they were in some Fortrillium installation at all times, he had to remember that.

Everything they saw could be touched. There was smell and texture – his senses were alive with the surroundings. The flames certainly seemed to exist, there was nothing about their sound and their heat that didn't feel real. Yet Joe understood that it was all a simulation. There was no trickery in the way Zach had died, though. He'd experienced the pain and terror for himself as he held on to his friend's hand.

The other Justice Seekers were beginning to move now. They'd sensed it was safe. As they brushed off the dirt and scanned the area for hazards, they began to stand up to breathe the fresher air.

It occurred to Joe that in spite of the smoke and flames the airflow had seemed strong. Even in his pit, as the flames roared all around them, the air had been stale, but present at least. Maybe this was how they were kept alive in The Grid. There was an audience to entertain on the screens after all.

Clay came over to Joe and put his arm on his shoulder by way of reassurance, as if he wanted to check it wasn't an illusion. Lucy was standing up with Chris who was calm and coherent. Joe wondered why he'd been placed in the Institution in the first place.

Two of the trenches lay undisturbed, the bodies still covered in dirt. Joe moved towards them with Clay. They brushed the dirt away and shook the Justice Seekers who'd taken shelter there.

Both were motionless and cold.

'They're dead,' said Clay, unnecessarily.

They'd lost two of the smugglers in white overalls, one of them a man – they didn't know his name – and the other the woman in their cell who wouldn't reveal her name to them. They hadn't been able to save these two Justice Seekers, they hadn't even had time to learn who they were. At least they were not alone when they died, they'd had other people to help them.

Joe scanned the surrounding environment. Any evidence of the fire was gone, and they were back in the greenery of a copse. Joe recalled wooded areas like this from his short time on Silk Road, but in The Climbs you grew accustomed to concrete.

He could hear water. His throat was dry and raw, the ashy smoke clung to his lungs like a thick fog. Nine of the Justice Seekers made for the stream, gulping down the fresh water and washing the sooty blackness from their hands and faces. Only Clay remained to cover the dead with dirt once again. These shallow graves would be all they could offer in The Grid.

Joe knew how it worked. They'd get a short period of respite to regroup and explore, then some new challenge would come along at night-time when the audiences for the screens were at their highest.

In the meantime, they'd show reruns of Zach's death. They'd replay the sequence where the inmates dug frantically in the soil to create the protective trenches and they'd hope for the group to become divided as leaders stepped forward and different factions were created from the survivors.

'Are you okay, Lucy?'

'Yes, fine. I needed that water, my throat felt like it was closing up.'

'I know what you mean. They don't want us all dead yet, there's usually a way to survive.'

'I'm so glad we've got Clay. I didn't know what to do when I saw the flames. I was useless.'

'Me too,' Joe admitted. 'They're going to spare you until the end, Lucy. You're too valuable to them. Always look for the way out. Until we get through the first set of Modes, there will always be a solution.'

Lucy nodded. They sat in silence for a while. There wasn't much to say – all of them needed a moment to process what had happened. Only one of the group was alert. It was the man in black overalls. The serial killer.

Joe watched him carefully. They'd have to remember that the dangers wouldn't only come from The Grid. This man was a potential threat too. He oozed contempt and indifference, but Joe wondered how he'd have survived without Clay having taken the initiative. Perhaps he needed them more than he knew.

They were down to ten people: Lucy, Clay, Joe, Chris, Marjani, Ross and Miron had all survived. There was the man in the black overalls, then another man and a woman – nobody knew who they were, they'd been part of a different group. The man wore white overalls, though it was difficult to tell what colour they should have been, they were so filthy from the trench.

The woman wore orange overalls – assault – another Justice Seeker with a violent background. Joe had to take care not to judge. They all had their stories to tell, nobody had seemed guilty of anything to him.

Except for the serial killer, he was worrying Joe.

'I'm Rick Stokley, thanks for your help there.'

The silence was broken. Rick extended his hand, to nobody in particular.

Another Justice Seeker from Silk Road – he'd offered a handshake. Joe felt there were more than usual in this trial. Clay rejoined the group.

'Good to have you here, Rick. What's your story?'

'Contraband!' he laughed. 'Smuggling supplies into The Climbs.'

It was the usual story for Joe. Fortrillium called it a crime, but to those who had to survive in The City, it was just humanity.

'I have family in The Climbs – I've been smuggling for years. What else can you do? I'm not leaving them on their own in there.'

'What about you?' Clay motioned to the woman in the orange overalls. She was reluctant to speak at first. She was aware of the camera drone overhead recording all the details of the conversation.

'I'm Grace,' she began at last. 'Grace Makins.'

The name was familiar to Joe.

'I'm in here for assault.'

'Care to explain why?' sneered the man in the black overalls.

'Most of you probably know why. 'I left one of the Centuria paralysed after beating him with an iron pole. It was well-publicized on the screens. I was a fugitive for over a month.'

Joe recalled the news story. She'd been the most wanted woman in The City at the time. Attacking the Centuria was not a good thing to do, it never ended well. They looked after their own. She'd been subjected to a horrific beating herself once they'd captured her.

'I bet you regret that now, don't you?' asked Clay.

'My only regret is that I only left him paralysed. I meant to kill him.'

They'd all seen enough of the Centuria to know what she meant. Nobody blamed her, they all felt enough contempt towards the Centuria to do the same themselves, given the provocation.

'How about you? Care to introduce yourself?'

Clay was talking to the man in the black overalls.

'You won't know me,' he replied. 'My kind of case is kept away from the screens, they like to hush it up.'

'You're a killer, right?' asked Ross.

'If you have to put it like that, yes, I suppose I am. My name is Schälen.'

'Is that your second name?'

Several of the Justice Seekers asked the question at the same time.

'Just call me Schälen, that's all you need to know.'

'Never heard a name like it,' said Miron. 'You from Silk Road or The Climbs?'

'I'm from The Climbs, but I like to frequent Silk Road.'

Joe thought his answers were more cryptic than useful, but at least he was speaking to them now. Schälen picked up on the questioning looks that were coming his way.

'I had a permit to work on Silk Road, only I didn't always do my job,' he smiled. 'Let's put it this way, I used a lot of my time on Silk Road to pursue an interest of mine. And, before you ask, it had nothing to do with charity.'

The way Schälen spoke unnerved Joe. Whatever he said seemed to drip with contempt and derision. He was not out to make friends, that was for sure. There was something remote and cold about him. Apart from the ridiculous name, he was the only person in the group who didn't seem to want to be a part of it.

The conversation moved on. The others felt the same about him, they didn't want to engage more than they had to. Clay took the initiative once again. He was generally accepted as the leader now, though Schälen wasn't responding directly to anybody, and kept his distance. He was listening to what was being said, but he didn't help at all, he just took care of his own needs.

Chris cowered when he was around, as though he emitted a dark force field. Joe resolved to watch Schälen carefully. They were safe at that moment, but he wasn't at all sure how he might behave if left alone with somebody. Chris seemed particularly vulnerable.

It was customary in The Grid to allow the Justice Seekers to fend for themselves. There was water from the stream, and if this trial followed the regular format there would be a source of food somewhere.

Clay organized the groups into teams to go foraging. They knew that further danger would not be far away. In fact, things might turn at any moment. But it was impossible to know when the next Mode would begin. There were still two more to come.

'Joe, Marjani, Ross, you head in that direction. Look for shelter, food, anything you can find.'

'How about weapons?' suggested Ross.

'Anything you can find.'

Clay sent out Miron, Rick and Grace in another direction.

'Lucy, how about you stay with Chris and me. Let's see if we can sort out a plan for Chris next time we get in a fix.'

Lucy nodded. The next Mode would not be far off, and

they needed to drill Chris to stop him getting into a panic. They'd have to coach him on what to do.

Clay didn't involve Schälen. He'd already indicated by his remote position in the group that he wasn't going to be a part of the scouting exercises.

It was beginning to get dark. Although The Grid was a completely artificial environment, the conventions of night and day would be preserved. The Justice Seekers would be given enough access to food and water, and there would be sufficient shelter, at least until they passed through the first Modes. After that, anything could happen.

Dusk brought the groups back together again. They'd had little success finding anything useful and it looked as if they were all going to go hungry that night.

The best bet seemed to be to settle down around the large tree next to the stream. They'd get shelter there and would be close to the water.

'Stay together,' Clay warned. 'Always tell somebody if you wander off. If they start a new Mode while we're separated, you're on your own. We're stronger if we work as a group.'

There was a general consensus on this point, and the members of the group settled down for the night. They'd been unable to light a fire so far, and there seemed little else to do.

Schälen was sitting on the ground leaning against a tree, some distance away from the main group: close enough to hear, but far enough not to be part of the conversation. He'd found something to eat, but they couldn't see what it was. He just sat there, surveying them. He was still watching as dawn broke. Already their numbers were depleted, but he knew he was strong enough to stay safe, until the end at least. Sure, his crimes were ugly, but that made him a great person to have as a Justice Seeker inside The Grid.

They called him a serial killer, but there was much more to it than that. He hated the word killer, he considered himself more of an artist. Every person he'd ever killed had been like painting a picture: starting with the idea, the rough sketch, then building up the layers, step by step.

The word 'killer' made what he did sound commonplace or ordinary. What he did to his victims was far from ordinary. His unique skill was in drawing out the moment of death. It fascinated him how much of the body you could actually remove and still keep a person alive. He'd have to improvise a little in The Grid, they could not provide him with his usual tools, not straight away, but he'd been told to make his first move as soon as possible. If he created tension and fear among the Justice Seekers, Fortrillium would keep him alive a little longer, that was the deal. They'd even given him a weapon, which he'd kept concealed.

The survivors from the fireball were tired and exhausted from their first challenge, in need of rest before the trial continued. They'd have to use the daytime to find food and shelter, plan their defence, and prepare for what came next. They were never safe, but the best trials came in the evening when more people in The City were gripped by what was playing out on the screens.

Now they thought they'd reached sanctuary, he'd make his first move and break off from the primary group. So far they were sticking together, but if past Justice Trials were anything to go by they'd be split up within the first twenty-four hours and pitted against each other.

He surveyed those who were left and wondered who he would pick as his first victim. This was the artist in him – a regular killer would not be so fussy. Then the decision was made for him. One of the women was getting up to explore the woodland environment. Lots of cover and many places to hide, just how he liked it. This would be his first masterpiece. He'd conceal her somewhere safe where he could work on her deliberately, allowing him to savour every one of her final minutes as he killed her, slowly, painfully, over a number of hours. They'd never even guess what was going on.

As Lucy got up quietly to scout around for food, he followed behind, exhilarated that his first kill would come so soon.

The Pact

Damien Hunter flicked through the browning pages of the document. He might just as easily have viewed it on his console, but at times like this he liked to review the original item.

He wondered what the world was like when this had been hurriedly written by a government which had virtually been wiped out. The world had been at a point where there was almost no rule at all. The plague had ravaged the entire planet, that much he knew from what he could piece together, and The City had been created from the ruins of a society that was gasping for life.

Little was chronicled about the history of The City. He knew it had been a sanctuary for those with some resistance to the plague. They had penned themselves in, and this document had given instructions about how this new society should be rebuilt.

He'd been in charge of Fortrillium for the past nine years. He knew from the dates of the signatures that it was almost a hundred years to the day since The City had been created.

Books were illegal under his rule, he'd been very particular about that. With knowledge came power, and if he was to save his family as much power as possible had to reside in his hands.

The problem was President Delman. He was the reason that Hunter was reading and rereading The Pact. The President had always been there – Hunter had never known a time without him. He'd been born in The City and Delman had been a perpetual presence, on the screens and in the news updates.

As Hunter had progressed swiftly through the ranks of Fortrillium, he'd become increasingly fascinated by Delman's position. He was not elected and he could not be removed. Succession was through death or illness. In spite of his age, Delman never seemed to falter. Hunter speculated that he must be in his eighties.

You could apply the word 'unknown' to a lot of things connected with President Delman. Damien had heard the rumours about him being the only person ever to have walked out of The Grid alive, but there was no proof. He'd tried to find it once, after gaining the position of Head of Fortrillium, but the evidence appeared to have been tampered with. There were no records. In spite of having the highest level of access to The City, he was unable to find out anything more about the President.

It was all the two men could do to hide their hostility towards each other. Delman had the upper hand in seniority, but Hunter would do everything he could to antagonize him.

The Pact was where Hunter turned for solace. He studied it hard, looking for any small space which might allow him to put additional pressure on the President. He'd even considered assassination at one point, but he knew how ridiculous that would be. This was the dichotomy of his leadership: he was paralysed by The Pact.

As a younger man he'd aspired to the role of leader – he'd even dared to conjecture there might be a way for him to become President one day. But just as Hannah had been surprised to find that the realities of becoming a Gridder were much harsher than she could ever have imagined, so it was for Hunter as leader of Fortrillium.

He was young to be offered the role, in his mid-thirties. He'd just demonstrated a skilled deployment of force and intimidation to quell a minor uprising in The Climbs, so he was very much the man of the moment.

The sudden death of his predecessor resulted in an impromptu visit to the President's office. Their relationship was a lot more cordial in those days, but it would never be the same again after that meeting.

All meetings like this tended to happen the same way. Damien knew nothing about it beforehand. He suddenly became aware of a vehicle following close behind, and immediately began to fear for his life. A shadowy figure had stepped out of the car, sent from the President's office.

Hunter had been summoned to meet with President Delman. There was to be no delay. He'd asked if he could go home first, to check in with his wife and kids, but that had been deemed 'unnecessary'. He still remembered the chill he'd felt when he'd heard those words, and it had proven to be justified. Delman had dispensed with all civility when they'd met. There was a sudden change in their relationship on that day, and it would only deteriorate from that point onwards.

It was at that meeting that Hunter saw The Pact for the

first time. It was sitting on the President's desk when he was escorted into the room.

Within the space of five minutes, Hunter received the best news and the very worst news that he could possibly hear. In the first minute of his conversation, he learned that he was to achieve his ambition of becoming the Head of Fortrillium. He effusively accepted the position – it made him cringe every time he thought about it. He'd been too quick to speak.

In the next four minutes of this short conversation, he would see his life crumble and turn to ruins.

Under The Pact, to ensure loyalty to the President, the Head of Fortrillium had to forfeit their family to the Umbilica. Only two people in The City knew what was in The Pact. Once viewed, the only way out was through death, such was its importance.

To ensure total compliance, Hunter had to sacrifice his family. They would rest in the Umbilica until his death: safe, protected and frozen in time. But he would never see them again. Their lives would only be preserved if he fulfilled his duties and obligations to The City.

He'd discovered that three minutes into his conversation with the President. Before four minutes were up, he found out that he had no choice in the matter. His family were in the Umbilica already, he would not be able to say his goodbyes. He had been chosen because of his undoubted skills of strategy and leadership. He was the man for the job, whether he wanted it or not.

To preserve the rule of the President, Fortrillium ran the security forces, but it was the President who was in overall charge. In any dispute, the President had the final say. If Hunter had dared to use the Centuria to attempt a coup, their own families would perish, swiftly and without mercy, as would Hunter himself.

For the Centuria, too, the small print of the job was never revealed beforehand. For each new recruit, their family members had their Gen-ID devices modified. If the strict rules of conduct weren't observed, their loved ones could be instantly terminated. Only Damien and the President could activate this – it ensured complete loyalty. At the press of a button, they could take the life of a Centuria and their family in seconds. It had served to preserve the integrity of the system for almost one hundred years. The new world needed order – without it humanity could perish.

Damien had pleaded with President Delman to allow his family to live by his side. Delman had refused his request.

In the fifth minute of the exchange, Delman had handed over a copy of The Pact. He'd declared that everything Hunter needed to know was in there. Hunter had been escorted from the room, sobbing, with the document in his hand. He would be taken to a secure area to read and digest the paperwork, and then escorted to his new office in the Fortrillium building where he would receive a full briefing.

People who knew the Hunter family would wonder what had happened to his lovely wife and children. They'd seemed such a happy family before he became Fortrillium's head. There was speculation about marital separation. Some gossiped that his family had been sent to The Climbs. In spite of the rumours, they all agreed on one thing. Damien Hunter changed on that day – he was never again the same man that they'd known before his family's strange disappearance. Something had broken him. They knew better than to ask, of course, and it wasn't long until he moved out of the neighbourhood anyway. It was one more unresolved matter in The City and another one soon forgotten.

Hunter understood that he'd changed on that day. He felt the hatred and the venom poison his body; he despised Delman and what he had done to his family. He was completely paralysed, there was nothing he could do. If he made a move to depose the President, his family would perish in the Umbilica. If he colluded with the Centuria on anything else but The City business, they'd all lose their families. It was checkmate.

There was no way to depose the President – under the constitution drawn up in The Pact, his rule was absolute. Yet nobody understood how he had been invested with that power. There was no challenge to be made.

If there was unrest in The Climbs, the Centuria would be forced to quash it. If they didn't comply, they and their families would perish.

If Hunter didn't issue the correct demands, he would lose his own family.

If Silk Roaders dared to make a stand they'd end up in The Climbs, along with their families.

And if those in The Climbs dared to protest, they'd wind up in The Grid. Everybody knew how that ended. At the centre of it all was a system designed to claim that there was justice, but which was used to silence any hope or resistance.

It was a city frozen by fear and the inability to act. And it all came to rest at the President's feet.

Hunter finished thumbing through The Pact, coming to an abrupt end at the back pages. The final three pages had been torn out, except for the last page right at the end. This one bore the signatures of the members of the government from the time of the plague who had passed this all as law. It was sealed with the official stamp and signature of the President at the time: James Morgan.

Hunter had asked once why the final pages were missing. They'd been removed after the heading 'Catharsis' and the beginning of a sentence outlining what was to happen at the first Centurial.

Delman had dismissed his query, claiming that the original creators had discarded those pages, deeming them unnecessary at their signing and sealing. Hunter knew there would be another reason, but he was unable to challenge further. Instead, he resolved to do everything within his very limited powers to get to the truth and be reunited with his family.

He'd waited nine years for this time. The Centurial was almost upon them – he was not privy to the specific date. Whatever was hidden in those documents would soon become evident. He was ready to act when it came – if there was an opportunity to strike, he would. He could sense President Delman's shadow behind him all the time – the two men had been trying to outmanoeuvre each other for years.

Hunter closed The Pact, returned it to his safe and activated the DNA locking system. He knew better than to let it fall into the wrong hands; that would result in his own death – probably in The Grid – and the death of his family.

He'd come so close to understanding what was going on when he'd discovered Matt Parsons' and Tom Slater's activities, but then Delman had closed off all routes to the truth. He'd never figured out how he managed that.

As soon as Hunter had received intelligence about the dubious activities of Joe Parsons and Lucy Slater, he immediately knew what it was connected with. Matt and Tom must have left a trail, one that Delman couldn't stop and probably didn't know about.

He suspected that he knew what Parsons and Slater had discovered – it was likely to be the same information that he sought himself. He'd thought for a while that he might have to do business with Talya Slater, but catching her kid red-handed in the sewers like that had been the best gift that she could give him. Her daughter and Parsons had done his work for him. He was the closest to the truth he'd ever been. He could punish Talya and still get the information that he needed, without Delman's involvement.

Hunter moved to the next item in his stack of paper. Funny how things came together. There he was thinking about Tom Slater again and here was the latest request from his wretched wife. Delman had played his hand well in making Talya a Law Lord and keeping her close to him at the time of the Centurial. And here she was, goading him once again with another legal request he couldn't refuse.

Not content with her tour of the prison system and operational areas of The Grid, Slater now wanted to meet the Gridders to learn for herself how the Justice Trials were created. She'd get her visit alright, he couldn't legally block it. But there was no way that she'd be leaving with even half of the truth. She'd hear what she needed to hear. And after-wards? He'd instruct the Gridders to make sure that some-thing very nasty happened to her daughter in The Grid ... a day or two before she was finished off for good.

Alliance

Talya woke early. She'd barely slept due to the tension of the trial. She'd gone to bed with Lucy and Joe still alive.

She'd been horrified as she watched the replays on her screen. So many lives lost already and to see Zach Fuller die in the flames like that ... Poor Joe, Zach had been like a father to all of them.

She wasn't sure how much more she'd be able to take. Perhaps if she couldn't save Lucy in time, she might give up then. But what about Joe, if he survived after Lucy's death? She'd had enough already, that was for sure. She was sickened by what she'd done to Max, yet it seemed insignificant compared with the horror of what Lucy and Joe were enduring.

Talya had an early meeting. She was due to meet Damien Hunter at Fortrillium – she'd requested an introduction to the Gridders. After what she'd learned from Max the night before, she felt sure she could help Lucy. She just needed a little more information.

Max had continued to make her life difficult after he'd regained consciousness. His hand had been torn apart by the knife ripping the flesh between his index and middle fingers. She'd found medical supplies in his house, nothing much, but she wished she'd had the same materials when she'd been trying to care for Harry earlier.

She was able to clean up and disinfect Max's wound; she stitched it and bandaged it as best she could. All the time she worked to heal him, she hated herself for what she'd done to him in the first place. Their relationship was like the bully to the victim; he was too scared to risk her anger, he just wanted to placate her so she'd leave him alone.

He was so scared of her that he'd flinch when she moved towards his hand. She tried to reassure him that she wasn't like that. She had to extract the information from him to save her daughter's life. What choice did she have?

As she finished tying the bandage securely on his hand, he'd actually thanked her. Talya was taken aback by that. He had every reason to curse her.

Max had realized early on that there was more to come, but he had to get his hand sorted first. His wound would draw attention at work. Although he was scared of Talya, he was terrified of being found out for sending the WristCom into The Grid. He'd awoken with that stark realization when he'd come round earlier.

He'd been caught by Talya – that was his own fault. It would be easier to work with Talya than to be discovered by the Centuria. He'd end up in The Grid if they found out what he'd done with the WristCom. He'd have been better off reporting it in the first place. Maybe it would have been safer to destroy it.

Anyway, he'd been careless, it was his own fault. Now he'd have to work with this woman. Maybe he should have made up his mind about that before he'd forced her to plunge the knife into his hand.

'What do you want me to do?' he asked as she put the medical supplies away in their box.

Talya was caught off-guard. Max seemed to want to be more helpful. Thank God. At last!

'Look, I'm sorry I did this to you. I have to do what I can to save my daughter, surely you understand that, don't you?'

Max had nodded, then hung his head, as if ashamed for not being more forthcoming in the first place.

'I was just scared of the Centuria. You know what it's like.'

They stared across the table at each other. Everybody in The City knew what it was like.

'I need to find a way to get that WristCom to Lucy and

Joe,' Talya had continued. 'If I can communicate with them directly, I think we can save them.

You don't need to do anything, Mr Penner – Max – just help me when the time comes, okay? I promise that nobody will find out what you did. I'll take full blame if it comes to that.'

Max had nodded once again and they'd parted.

Talya knew she'd need to check in with Wiz and Mitchell, but wanted to catch up with the trial progress first.

Relieved that Lucy and Joe were still alive, she'd received more good news when the notification on her WristCom came in that her presence was required for Law Lord duties. That would be the next Mode in The Grid – they always began with an address from Damien Hunter in the presence of the Law Lords.

She'd been absent from the first appearance so she could pay her visit to Max, and Talya thought it best not to miss this one. Lucy would want to see her, she'd wonder why she wasn't there. Did Lucy even know she was a Law Lord? They hadn't spoken about it yet. She'd looked too drugged up and vague when she'd come in for sentencing with Joe – she didn't look as if she'd seen Talya sitting there among the Law Lords.

Talya went into Lucy's room to search in the drawer by her bed. She didn't like to invade her daughter's privacy, but she was looking for something. There was not much in there: handwritten notes from Hannah – that was to be expected, as the two were friends; pressed flowers, memorabilia of her father – Talya remembered the day they'd done that when Lucy was eight –, and the photograph of her dad she'd cut out from his Fortrillium identity card after his death.

Then she found it: the pendant. It had belonged to Talya's great-grandmother, who knew of life before the plague. She'd worried they were losing their history, and wanted the item to be passed down through future generations.

'We must remember,' she said before her death. 'If nobody can remember, we have no past.'

After Tom died, Talya gave the pendant to Lucy. She used it to help to console her.

'We must remember,' she'd repeated as Lucy wept on her bed, 'if nobody can remember, we have no past.'

Lucy had learned the lesson well. It was why she was in The Grid. She'd never forgotten her father or the sense of injustice at his death. She and Joe were bound together by a quest for vengeance.

Talya would wear the pendant at the beginning of the next Mode. If Lucy saw it, she'd know they were working to protect her and Joe. It was a sign of security for her.

She thought about Wiz and Mitchell – they'd need to meet up as soon as possible. They had to pull their plan together before the start of the next Mode.

She cursed her need for sleep. She'd been so exhausted by the events of the day before – with Harry's injuries, Lucy's arrest, the beginning of her Law Lord duties, it had all happened so quickly. She'd found herself in the middle of a nightmare.

Talya cleaned herself up and changed her blood-soaked clothes. She thought back to Max and hoped he'd remain steady. He was more scared of the Centuria. She thought he'd be fine.

She messaged Mitchell via her WristCom. He'd been quiet all night, and she was surprised he hadn't checked in. She understood that Wiz couldn't make contact, but they'd have that sorted out soon if Mitchell had got the right tech. Damn Mitchell for not checking in, she'd have words next time she saw him.

Talya understood what she needed to achieve that day. It would have to be accomplished by 19:30. That was the time she'd been given to meet with the other Law Lords. It would be the beginning of the next Mode, which would follow at 20:00 hours.

Escape for the Justice Seekers would not be so easy this time around. The trial had only been allocated three Modes, so Hunter and his team would want more deaths in the next round. Hunter would need the Justice Seekers thinned out before the final Mode and prior to Ascension. Talya felt sure he'd keep them alive until then. He'd want to goad her as long as possible, but it was likely that even Hunter couldn't guarantee a life in that wretched place.

Talya would get her heavily doctored tour of the Gridder facility, chase up Mitchell and Wiz, then liaise with Max once again. If they were really lucky, they'd be able to get a signal undetected to the WristCom. If they could do that, there was a chance they could get messages to Joe and Lucy.

Talya placed the pendant into her pocket, threw her bag over her shoulder and headed out of the house. It was going to be another long day. She walked along the road towards Fortrillium's imposing headquarters, her mind distracted by thoughts of Lucy and the risks they were going to have to take. Had she been a little less preoccupied, she might have noticed Teanna Schaelles following close behind, out of sight, but on her tail.

CHAPTER FOUR

Resistance

Wiz felt a sudden urge to leap off the side of the tower block. With three Centuria pointing their weapons at him, things were unlikely to play out well.

He was about to make a run for it when one of the Centuria dropped his weapon and pulled off his helmet. He held out his hand.

'Leo Bachus. That was a close call.'

Wiz stared at him. He'd never been offered a handshake in The Climbs before. People there tended to have more interest in where their next meal was coming from.

Leo realized his mistake and apologized.

'I'm sorry, I should have thought.'

The other Centuria lowered their weapons but remained helmeted.

Wiz studied Leo. He was young, not much older than he was. The Centuria were always anonymous, their helmets protecting their identities – it tended to keep things simpler in civilian life. It was difficult to stay friends with the neighbours if you'd arrested somebody on their street and they ended up in The Grid.

'There's no need to be afraid, we're not going to hurt you, Shen.'

They knew his name. Not the one he liked to use. Wiz guessed they were all searching for him.

'Call me Wiz. I never use Shen Li. It died with the rest of my family.'

'No problem. Do you want to put your bag down, Wiz? You've had a bit of a fright.'

Wiz put his bag down.

'Why do they have their helmets on?' he asked.

'I don't have family, Wiz. I'm like you, they're all dead. One of my friends here has family; she has more than just her own life to lose, she needs to hide her identity for now. I took mine off as a sign of trust, Wiz. You can trust us, we won't harm you.'

Wiz wasn't so sure. He'd rather have seen their faces.

One of the other Centuria spoke. It was a woman's voice. That startled Wiz; he'd never thought there might be women concealed beneath the masks. Brutality wasn't just a device used by men, he knew that, but it still surprised him to hear a young female speaking.

'Leo, we need to move fast. They'll want an update soon.'

'Okay, okay Jody. You're right. Let's get things moving.'

Jody removed her helmet – she felt it might help ease the tension a bit. Unlike her friend, she had no family to worry about.

'Wiz, we're a small group of Centuria looking for our chance to strike back at Fortrillium. There aren't many of us. The Centuria are controlled by fear and threats just like everybody else. We've been trying to track you down since the arrest alert went out – we want to work with you.'

Wiz wasn't so sure about that. Yet they'd saved his life already, he was still breathing.

There was a sound on the WristComs of all three Centuria, and the third spoke. It was another woman, she also sounded young.

'Leo, we need to give a report.'

'Jody, I'm going to step behind the aerials with Wiz. You file a full video report to HQ and tell them I'm checking the top five floors with Julia.'

'Will do,' she replied. 'Julia, send a follow-up report from two floors down in five minutes – confirm that the top five floors are clear.'

Julia hesitated, then moved off.

Wiz and Leo moved out of the way of Jody's camera, and Jody replaced her helmet before filing the report.

'What's with all the youngsters?' asked Wiz. He'd been surprised at how young everybody sounded.

'We have less to lose. The Centuria with partners and children, they're much less likely to risk joining us, even if they want to. Julia has lots of family on Silk Road; her hand was forced when she joined us – sometimes you have to take sides. Jody is like me, no family.

'We met in the Centuria, got talking on long overnight shifts. We all think the same way: there needs to be change in The City. We have to move carefully, though. If they discover us, it'll be the shortest resistance movement in history.'

'Wiz, I'm going to give you a WristCom. It's not secure yet, you'll need to get it reconfigured, but it won't be traced. It's from a dead man.'

Leo handed the device to Wiz, who hoped it wasn't an omen.

'A clever guy like you can get this fixed. I've read your profile.

I want you to carry on what you're doing here; we know this rig must be connected to whatever you were doing in the sewers.'

'Don't tell me what it's for now. If they catch us, it's better that we don't know. But if you need help, get that WristCom sorted and give us a call. We're stationed in The Climbs for the next two weeks of shifts – that should easily cover your friends' trial and whatever you're up to. We're all in this together, Wiz, and if we can help you, we will.'

He held out his hand again but withdrew it immediately. Wiz didn't need any more reminders of the differences between them.

Wiz concealed the WristCom in his pocket. Whatever Leo and his friends were up to, they had just saved his life and given him the most useful piece of equipment he could have asked for. It wasn't a bad start to a new alliance. He didn't even have to share any information with Leo; it seemed a safe bet. He'd discuss it later with Talya, see what she thought.

Leo could hear Jody finishing off her status update to Fortrillium. He placed his helmet back on his head. Immediately he looked more sinister and threatening.

Wiz and Leo walked around the corner when Jody had signed off.

'We're leaving now, Wiz. We'll report this area clear. Finish off whatever you're doing and get out of here – there won't be any new patrols in Pegasus block tonight.'

Wiz nodded and watched as Leo and Jody left the rooftop.

He looked around for his bag so he could start work on the aerials once again. He'd move around to the other side of the scaffold; it had looked more secure there when he'd been speaking to Leo. He scolded himself for not having taken more care the first time.

As he picked up his bag, a thought struck him. His new Centuria friends were away, it was too late to call back to them. Only minutes previously he'd heard Jody signing off her video update and reporting that all was clear at the top of the tower block. She'd had her camera pointing towards the edge of the rooftop, exactly where Leo had taken his hand earlier and pulled him to safety. But she'd overlooked something. His bag must have been visible on the video feed. It was right there, aerials and all, just waiting to be spotted by Fortrillium.

Missing

Joe woke in a sweat. He'd had a broken sleep, teased all night with thoughts of the past forty-eight hours.

In his dreams Lucy had fallen from the cage. Clay had almost caught her, but he'd lost his grip and she'd plunged to her death on the hard floor below. He'd been too indecisive; when Lucy had needed him, he hadn't been there.

He'd jumped out of his sleep as her body hit the ground. It was still dark, everybody else was still. Eventually he drifted back to sleep, but the nightmares continued.

This time, it was Zach. Joe was holding his hand as his blistered body burned in front of him. In the dream, Joe couldn't release the hand. Zach's body writhed and contorted as he was tortured by the fire, and all he could do was to hold on. As Zach's body finally went limp, he kept saying the same words over and over again to Joe.

'You could have saved me if you'd tried harder ... You could have saved me if you'd tried harder ... '

Joe woke again. It was light, or at least getting there. The others were beginning to move now. He dozed a short time, thinking about what lay ahead of them.

Things would change soon; their present environment would be moved on to suit whatever trial challenge was coming next. It could be anything. Joe knew enough about The Grid to understand there was no point trying to guess. The horrors inflicted upon the Justice Seekers were as diverse as the minds which devised them. There was no point worrying. The Mode would change at a time of Fortrillium's choosing. They needed to eat, stay strong and work together. The trials always lasted longest with a strong leader and a team which stuck together.

Joe looked over towards Schälen, but he wasn't there. He was nervous about that man. Joe had seen it before. The commentators of the screens called them 'wild cards'. 'Sociopaths' would have been a more accurate description.

Every now and then you'd get someone like Schälen thrown into a trial. There weren't a lot of people like him in The City – most crimes were related to survival and self-preservation. Schälen's crimes were vindictive and violent. They had nothing to do with staying alive, they were motivated by a hatred for humanity. That made him dangerous and unpredictable.

The other Justice Seekers just wanted to survive. They all knew how the trials ended, yet there was still that glimmer of hope every time. You could see it on the faces of whoever was in The Grid. They should have all given up in the first Mode, but they kept fighting and fighting. Even when all seemed lost, they would continue to fight. Joe understood it now he was there. He knew that none of them were getting out of The Grid, it was an evil game run by Fortrillium. But like all the others, he would fight until the end. He refused to lie down and die.

Their leader was Clay – he was strong and knew what to do. More of them would be dead already if it hadn't been for Clay; he'd saved lives and shown he could make quick decisions. They all accepted it too. There was no doubt that Clay would lead them as far as they were going to go in this trial. They had two Modes left, two more challenges before the final trial.

They'd done well. At least the end would not be far off. If they'd drawn ten Modes, it might have gone on for weeks. Joe wasn't sure he could have taken that. You tired quickly in The Grid; he'd seen ten-Mode trials when all of the Justice Seekers had been dead by the halfway point. The second Mode was likely to follow that evening, and they'd need to be ready when it came.

Joe looked over to Clay. He was still lying on the ground, his eyes open. He saw that Joe was gazing in his direction and smiled.

'You okay, Joe?'

'Yes, bad dreams, though.'

'Me too. I don't think any of us are getting sweet dreams in here.'

Joe laughed. He liked that Clay could make him smile, even in that terrible place. They sat up in silence for a while. Some of the others were still sleeping.

Joe wondered what Wiz and Mitchell were up to. They were taking their time. Surely they'd get a message to him and Lucy soon; he had to trust that they were still free and working on the data they'd discovered.

He cursed that they'd been caught. They knew the risks, they always had. If only they'd had a little more time.

Joe hoped his friends would be working hard to secure their release – it was the only way they were walking out of The Grid alive.

He hadn't even considered how the information might be used. He'd been so intent on trying to find what his father was doing. There had never really been a big plan. They'd not thought much further than hacking in and getting to the truth.

And what of Hannah? They hadn't heard from Hannah in a couple of days. Joe didn't even know if she'd been successful in the contest. Would she be able to help, even if she'd got closer to the Gridders? He didn't know, none of them knew what would happen if Hannah won, they just had their theories. Nobody outside Fortrillium really knew how The Grid operated – it was all conjecture.

Joe tried to lift his spirits. He was desperate to find out what was going on back in The City. Surely, Talya would be working on their behalf too ... they wouldn't just be abandoned there. Would they?

'We need to think about food.'

Clay's voice brought Joe out of his brooding. It was easier for the people who lived in The Climbs, they were used to doing without. Having no food for a few days was never easy, but they'd all done it at one time or another. The Silk Roaders would struggle though; they'd soon weaken without meals.

There was always a way to eat in The Grid, but Fortrillium didn't make it easy. Justice Seekers usually had to look to the environment for the solution. They'd been placed in a wood, and they had water nearby. It wasn't close enough to save Zach, but at least they'd been able to drink. Joe thought back to the fire the night before; he could still taste the dirt from the trench and the smoke in his mouth.

Joe looked over at Chris. He was chatting to Miron and Ross and seemed much more settled, certainly less anxious. Why had he even been sent to the Institution? He seemed fine.

Then it clicked. Where was Lucy? She'd gone to sleep close to Chris, but she wasn't there anymore. Joe sat up and looked around the group. Marjani and Rick, but no Lucy.

'Anybody seen Lucy?

Did she go to the stream?'

There were blank looks all round.

'Chris?'

Chris looked guilty, as if he'd forgotten all about his friend, the person who had immediately taken him under her wing and protected him. He hung his head but did not reply.

'Lucy!' Joe shouted. He thought she might have gone looking for food – as a Silk Roader she'd have been feeling the hunger.

'Lucy!'

No answer. Joe looked over to where Schälen had taken shelter for the night.

'Have you seen her, Schälen?' he called.

Schälen shrugged.

'We need to find her,' Clay began. 'We must stay together for when they change the Modes.'

'I don't trust Schälen,' Joe muttered. 'He's going to be trouble.'

'Forget him for now, focus on Lucy.'

Clay had a knack of being able to see what needed to be done. Those who were sitting stood up and they split off into informal groups. It struck Joe how much their numbers were already depleted. He needed to find Lucy; he was angry with her for walking off unannounced.

As Clay started to send out the search parties in their separate directions, they were suddenly surrounded by darkness. The morning light, which had seemed such a positive start to the day, was gone. Joe wondered if this were another of his bad dreams – perhaps he'd imagined that Lucy had disappeared. This was real, though – it went icy cold as soon as the light disappeared.

'Clay? You still there?'

'I'm here. Stay still everybody!'

'Hell, they're changing the Modes already,' Ross cursed.

'Give us a breather, won't you?' he shouted out.

Joe felt rapid breathing by his side, a menacing presence, but it was too dark to see who it was.

'Get ready everybody – here comes our next treat.'

It was Schälen. He'd moved over from his tree some distance away to join the main group. Joe shivered, but this time it wasn't the cold. How had Schälen done that? It was way too dark to move.

'Lucy!' called Clay. 'Where are you?'

No reply. Just silence and blackness.

'If she gets caught in the Mode change it could kill her.'

Miron's voice cut through the darkness. Joe knew what it meant: they needed to be in the circle when it changed.

'Lucy!' he called again, but he knew it was useless. Wherever she was, it wasn't within shouting distance. He felt himself beginning to panic; the rising sense of anxiety was shocking to him. It wasn't helped by Chris who'd begun to sob again. He understood what was coming.

A light appeared in the darkness. Joe and Clay looked around, making sure they were all together and hoping to see Lucy. It was the holographic image of Damien Hunter. Joe felt the snarl as he spoke.

'Justice Seekers, you have survived the first Mode in your quest for justice.'

Ross threw a stone at the projected image. Joe only saw it as it flew into the light, but it made him want to laugh. He tried to master his feelings – he knew it was just a reaction to the fear.

'Now you must move into the second Mode.'

'Here it comes ...'

It was Marjani's voice.

'Stay close everybody.'

More reassurance from Clay, just when they needed it.

'Don't worry, I will.'

Schälen's voice again. The man couldn't speak without it sounding as if he was about to tear your throat out.

'The way of The Grid is to take an eye for an eye, a tooth for a tooth, a life for a death.

May you find your justice in The Grid ...'

The light was back again, albeit very dim. Joe had a moment to take everything in. The woodland was gone. He could no longer hear the water from the stream. They were in a dark tunnel. The only available light was given off by the flames of the burning torches lining the walls.

There was the roar of a beast from deep within the maze of passages. It was like nothing they'd ever heard before. Then a scream. A human scream. It was Lucy's voice. And it came from the same direction as the creature.

The Second Mode

Hannah had barely had any rest before they were roused from their brief sleep. When she'd arrived for her first day at Fortrillium, she hadn't anticipated becoming incarcerated there while the trial took place. She hadn't even expected to become an integral part of the trial so early.

Her fellow Gridders were full of praise for her. She'd set them off to an excellent start. But it was all through gritted teeth – they knew it only increased the pressure on the rest of them. The stress was palpable.

She hoped her parents knew what was going on. Hunter had assured her they'd been informed, but being kept away from home was not something she'd planned for.

There were many rumours about the Gridders. Nobody knew who they were, and it was believed that they walked among the inhabitants of Silk Road. They were only known on the screens by their gaming names, and as such they became celebrities if they made dramatic kills. Already, the buzz over this latest trial was about Janexx2. Hannah didn't know it, and the residents of The City would never discover her true identity. The City had observed the work of this new Gridder and they understood that this trial was going to be fierce.

97TRaider joined Hannah for food, and she felt relieved at least to have somebody available to talk her through what was going on.

'Why are we up so early?'

'That's my doing, sorry. If you hadn't made such a good start last night, I'd have gone a little softer on them. I've decided to change the Mode early. They won't be expecting it.'

Hannah looked at 97TRaider.

'Did you sleep last night?'

'I skipped it, I've been working on my gameplay all night. They won't want the engagement score to drop now. I'm afraid you set the bar a bit high.'

'Sorry, but I'm new to all this, you know!' Hannah snapped at him.

'Woah! Take it easy. I'm not the enemy here.'

'Sorry. I'm just a bit tense.'

'I understand, but if you think it's bad now, wait until we get past the Modes and on to Ascension. It becomes unbearable.'

Hannah doubted herself once again. Was she really up to this? It had seemed so easy when plotting with Lucy, Joe and the others. Now she hadn't heard from them in days, and she wouldn't be able to see them until the Justice Trial was over.

They'd never anticipated what it would be like when they decided to get her in among the Gridders. She felt foolish when she recalled how she'd just thought it would be like a Fortrillium office job. How much more wrong could she have been?

'What have you got planned for today?'

'Well, I hope you don't mind, but I've requested a team play with you. We both get to count the kills. I thought it would be a great way for you to cut your teeth.'

Hannah looked at the piece of food on her fork and didn't feel like eating anymore. That feeling of sickness was back in her stomach. She was already responsible for three deaths. Three faceless people for her, just pixelated images. But, nevertheless, three human beings from The City. And now she was going to have to kill more.

'What's the gameplay?' she asked, deciding not to eat any more food. She'd need to get through that day on an empty stomach if she wasn't going to let herself down again.

'It's a labyrinth,' 97TRaider began, his eyes lighting up. 'They're going underground, in darkness, and I've put something nasty down there.'

'You do get that we're killing people, don't you?' Hannah snapped at him again.

'Shh!' he urged. 'Look, I know, but what can we do? I bet you came here like me, thinking that you'd just create and play a few games and then see yourself idolized throughout The City?'

'Not quite, but I wasn't expecting it to be like this.'

'Well, neither was I. Nobody thought it would be like this, but here we are. If I could get out of it, I would – but I can't. Neither can you, by the way. You make your kills and you don't leave until you do.'

Hannah knew that 97TRaider was right, but he'd had much more time to get used to it. She was trapped, they all were.

'These people will die anyway, it won't stop when we get out of here.'

Hannah nodded – she didn't like it, but it was true.

'At least we can finish them fast. I never let them linger. The kindest thing we can do is to make it swift and dramatic. That way Fortrillium gets what it wants and the Justice Seekers make a fast exit.'

He was right. 97TRaider had been on the same emotional journey as her. All of the Gridders must have reconciled it in a similar way. You'd have to be crazy for it not to bother you. But Fortrillium had them cornered. You always felt cornered in The City, whoever you were. It didn't make much difference whether you lived on Silk Road or in The Climbs.

That's why she'd taken on this challenge in the first place. Lucy, Joe, Wiz and Mitchell all had their tech skills, but nobody could get close to her when it came to gaming. Wiz and Joe didn't have that luxury in The Climbs, but

Mitchell and Lucy wouldn't have been able to take her place – they simply didn't have her level of ability. It had to be her. They'd all committed to this, it had been part of the plan.

Maybe she wasn't alone after all. 97TRaider seemed to be somebody she could trust – maybe he could become an ally?

'You're right,' she conceded. 'I know you're right. I wish I'd thought about that too – it makes sense to go for a fast kill. I don't know what I was thinking when I used fire, it's a terrible way to die.'

'We all make mistakes like that. Try not to let it eat you up, because it will if you let it.'

'It is eating me up already. I thought if I killed the first Justice Seeker in the fire the others would figure out how to make it out alive.

Fortrillium would get their big dramatic start and the others would get away.'

'Not bad thinking, Janexx2 ...'

97TRaider paused and searched Hannah's face. He wondered if he could trust her.

'Can we use real names?' he asked. 'You mustn't tell anybody if we do.'

Hannah looked back at him. Could she trust this person? He seemed honest – it was he who'd made the suggestion, after all.

'I'm Linwood Carley. Care to share your real name? If you do, we've made a pact, we can't undo it.'

Hannah's mouth opened before she'd even decided to share her name. She figured that she needed help if she was going to navigate the dangers of Fortrillium, and 97TRaider had already shown himself to be a friend.

'Hannah James!' she said quietly. 'I'll keep my mouth

shut, don't worry, I've already heard enough about this place to scare the life out of me.'

Linwood chuckled at that.

'We live in fear here – it's how Damien Hunter likes it.

But don't worry, Hannah, you can trust me. We'll both be in trouble now if they know we shared real names. Just make sure you don't slip up, always use 97TRaider.'

Hannah nodded and asked what he had planned for the labyrinth.

'We have to make some fast kills. They only have a three-Mode trial, and we don't want too many Justice Seekers in at the end when we move to Ascension. I reckon we need at least three kills, maybe even four. It's going to have to be good today.'

Hannah's heart sank, and she was pleased she hadn't eaten any more food. She felt sick all the time, it was the thought of what they had to do.

'Can we make them fast then if we have to kill?'

'Yes. This is going to be good, Hannah. Fortrillium will love it. I've created four beasts in the labyrinth; they're all contained at the moment.

I need to do a bit more rendering work on them – I need your help on that. We need to scare the life out of the people watching on the screens.'

For a moment, Hannah was distracted by a sense of excitement. The gamer in her saw the potential for this scenario. She checked herself – these were real people they were planning to kill.

'They're in the labyrinth right now. I put them in early while they weren't expecting it; it'll confuse them and frighten them. But here's the thing, Hannah. Something great happened last night.

We've got a psycho in there – did you read the profile notes?'

Hannah had. She'd clocked it too, but stored it up for later. A psycho might come in handy for some later gameplay.

'Last night he abducted one of the Justice Seekers, a female. He separated her from the main group – I think he had plans to torture her.

'Normally she'd have got caught when we re-rendered The Grid for the second Mode, but I saved her for later. I've put her right at the heart of the labyrinth. She's going to be the first to die, Hannah. The beasts will get her first, and then they'll start on the others.'

CHAPTER FIVE

Glimpse

Talya had an uneasy feeling that somebody was following her, but every time she stopped to check there was nobody to be seen. In the end she put it down to her paranoia. There was a lot going on, and she'd scared herself by what she'd done to Max. Although there was no way that anybody could possibly have known how she'd tortured him, her own sense of morality goaded her. She felt she deserved to be caught and punished.

Talya went through Fortrillium's security checks and was surprised to hear that Damien Hunter would be escorting her to her meeting with the Gridders – she thought he'd want to stay out of her way. But the lawyer in her saw an opportunity. They were like one of her warring couples, spiteful and vindictive, trying to get the better end of the settlement deal on a marriage break-up. In such cases, she always urged negotiation and dialogue. Would it work with Hunter? She would try. An opportunity to talk about things away from the public gaze might be what they both needed.

While she was waiting for Damien, Talya checked her WristCom for trial updates. She got her second shock of the day. The Modes had changed, Lucy had gone missing, and the Justice Seekers were in some sort of labyrinth. This was all news to her since she'd eaten breakfast. Talya hadn't expected that – she thought they'd be safe until 20:00 hours. Her mind raced as she thought about what might be happening to Lucy. How had she gone missing? What did that mean? At least the updates confirmed that there had been no further deaths. She cursed Hunter but resolved to keep her anger in check. If she could open an exchange of ideas with him, perhaps she could help Lucy. At least she was in the right place to see how The Justice Trials operated. She was going to meet the Gridders very soon.

Damien Hunter arrived, late as usual.

'Law Lord Slater, good morning!'

He greeted her as if it was just a normal day at the office. He held her daughter's life in his hands; she wanted to beat him to death.

'Good morning, Mr Hunter ...'

'Call me Damien, please. We should be on first name terms now you work with Fortrillium.'

'Damien then. Good morning. Thank you for agreeing to show me around this morning.'

'It's no problem at all, Talya – may I call you Talya?'

If this man were not her enemy, he would be extremely charming. Talya wondered if she might warm to him if the circumstances were different.

'Of course, Damien. I'd welcome a thawing in our relationship now we're working together.'

'I'm sure you would.'

There it was, the assertion of power once again. He couldn't stop playing the games, it seemed to be in his blood.

'Enough of that, though. Let's move on with the tour. It won't take long, there's not much to see.'

Damien touched his WristCom to alert the Gridder team of his imminent arrival. Talya guessed that was only for her benefit. Just like the prison visit, she knew this would be staged once again. They were probably all clearing their screens at that moment so she didn't see anything too informative as she toured the offices.

'Before you enter the Gridder facility, you'll need to sign some additional documentation.'

'No problem, Damien. What does it cover?'

'As a legal expert you'll understand the need for confidentiality, Talya.'

It struck her how strange it was to be using first name terms when all they both wanted to do was kill each other. All that cordiality and hate, what a potent cocktail it was.

'I do,' replied Talya. 'What does this concern?'

'The real names of Gridders must stay out of the public domain; their anonymity is a crucial part of our justice system.'

'Understandably, yes.'

'Should you recognize anybody among the Gridders today, you must not acknowledge your relationship inside this building, or outside it. Neither may you discuss Gridder-related matters with anyone unless it is part of closed-door Fortrillium business.'

'Understood,' said Talya. 'I apply the same constraints to any legal work and would expect to do so for any Law Lord related business.'

'Excellent, then please sign here, if you would.'

Damien held out an electronic tablet on which was

displayed the documentation they'd discussed. Talya took some time to read it. Good job she read right down to the bottom of the page – the punishment for collusion or conspiracy was imprisonment, and in extreme circumstances, trial in The Grid. Damien Hunter liked to enforce the rules, that was sure.

She had no choice but to sign. It seemed barely relevant to her by that stage. She didn't really care what happened to her if Lucy perished in The Grid. She was taking things to their final conclusion. She'd be cautious and diplomatic all the time Lucy was in The Grid. If she died, she'd take no prisoners. Talya had it all planned out. If Lucy lost her life, she'd seek out Damien Hunter and kill him immediately. No discussion, no warning, no long speeches. Just death, fast and final. She'd do it with a knife if she had to, but if she could get her hands on a gun that might help to get the job done better. Then she'd release a video message to the news organizations revealing everything she'd discovered.

She wasn't sure what would happen next. Would she kill herself before they caught her? Would she let herself become a spectacle for Fortrillium on the screens? She'd be going to the slaughter if she did. Suicide might be the preferable option. If she killed Hunter, she'd be a dead woman anyway. Talya wasn't sure how it would play out in the end.

Either way, she had to sign the document. It took a DNA sample as she signed too. That was standard practice with important contracts. Especially the type that could get you killed.

'Step this way please,' said Damien as he began to escort Talya towards the Gridder Complex. She wondered if he could sense that she was plotting how to kill him. She smiled to herself when she realized he was probably doing exactly the same thing.

As they walked along the bland corridors of Fortrillium, she was astonished to see they were alone. The usual Centuria escort was nowhere to be seen. Hunter would know he was safe all the while Lucy was alive, but he was not a stupid man. If Lucy died, would she get that close to him again? Probably not. Talya wondered if she'd have been better killing him there and then, with her hands. She decided to talk instead. They'd never actually conversed like sensible human beings.

As they entered a long, empty corridor, Talya stopped.

'Can we talk a moment, Damien ... confidentially?'

He looked at her, examining her face. He hadn't expected that.

'Of course, Talya. I think it's probably overdue, don't you?'

Where would she begin? There was so much that she wanted to scream at him. She needed to think of Lucy.

'How did it come to this, Damien? I'm not so dangerous to you, am I?'

Once again, Damien had not expected her to go directly to the main issue.

'We are where we are, Talya. Unfortunately, we're all subject to different pressures and we have to make the best decisions.'

'But did you have to involve Lucy? Did you really have to get the youngsters involved?'

'They got themselves involved, Talya. They were hacking into Fortrillium's systems, and you know we can't allow that.'

'I know, I understand, but couldn't you have talked to

me then, before you arrested Lucy? We could have come to an arrangement; it didn't have to play out like this.'

Damien looked carefully at her again. He was attempting to work out what kind of a person he was dealing with. She was right, it might have served him better to have talked. If he'd been a little less keen to hurt her, Lucy and Joe Parsons might have been more useful to him. It was too late, though. He'd managed to salvage their data and equipment, though it hadn't been a tremendous amount of help to him so far.

'I agree, Talya. Maybe we both could have been a little more friendly towards each other. But you made an enemy of Fortrillium a long time ago. You really could have helped us a bit more when you gave your interviews on the screens. You're a very influential woman you know, and influence can be used in a number of different ways.'

He was right, of course. In her rush to annoy and antagonize him, she'd been very negative about Fortrillium. Her anger was so great after Tom's disappearance, she'd never really thought about working alongside Fortrillium, rather than fighting them all the way.

'Is there anything I can do to help Lucy? You do understand how important this is, don't you? Do you have children of your own Mr Hunter? Damien?'

His face looked suddenly pale and drawn. She'd never heard his family mentioned, and she'd hit a sensitive spot by the look of him.

'I did have a family, Talya, but like you my work in The City comes with many obligations, some of them tough to bear.'

He hadn't given her a straight answer. She decided to push him a bit more.

'Do you have children, Damien? Surely you can understand what I'm going through?'

'I understand exactly what you're going through, Law Lord Slater, but you and your daughter brought it upon yourselves!'

He snapped at her. His face was red and he looked flustered. She'd never seen him that way before. He was on the defensive, she'd rattled him. There was a way to hurt Damien Hunter and it was through his family.

Talya resolved to get Wiz and Mitchell working on some research. She would talk to Delman about it too. Surely he would be able to tell her more about Hunter's family?

'I'm sorry if I touched on a sensitive matter, Damien. I didn't mean to. But if there's some way you can think of that would help us to resolve this issue, I want you to know that I am receptive to it.'

Hunter was struggling to regain his composure. He realized he'd given something away to Talya. He'd been taken by surprise when she asked him about his family – he never had conversations which dealt with personal matters. There was not much room in Fortrillium business to accommodate a family life.

'You of all people know the law of The City, Talya. Perhaps we should have had this conversation earlier, but our courses are fixed now, and there's nothing I can do to save your daughter. She may yet step out of The Grid and win her Justice Walk, but once she enters there is only one way out.'

Talya nodded. She'd just seen a glimpse of humanity in a man she'd believed to be inhuman. It could be they were both at fault, they'd both been in a rush to hurt each other. She thought about the couples she dealt with when handling marital disputes. It was always the same: rage, anger and pride prevented any reasonable discourse. Perhaps she had been guilty of doing exactly what she counselled her clients to avoid.

But then the anger surged through her once again. Hunter's was the original sin; it was he who had killed Tom and Matt. If Hunter had shown more mercy, maybe none of the events that followed would have taken place.

Talya and Damien stood in silence. Each had experienced an unguarded moment with the enemy, but it changed nothing.

They were both set on a course and it would have to play out in full. There was no turning back for either of them; it would inevitably end in death. But which of them would be left standing?

Visit

Hannah was working furiously at her console when the alert came around. She and Linwood had taken two of the creatures each. They were making them as fearsome as they could and allowing their imaginations to run free.

Hannah found the work incredibly absorbing, and she had to continually remind herself they were creating monsters which would be slaughtering human beings. Fortrillium had been clever disassociating the Gridders from the human element of the operation. At every turn, she was striving to make the gameplay better, and if she became too absorbed in her console work she forgot they were creating killing machines.

They'd been instructed to clean up their consoles and conceal any paperwork. A Law Lord was making a spot-check visit. They were not to discuss any details of the trial or their plans for the different Modes. They were reminded of the clause in their contracts which dealt with what they were – and were not – permitted to discuss. Their memories were also refreshed on the consequences if they were to disobey.

Hannah ensured her console was showing nothing confidential, then walked over to Linwood.

'I've had an idea for the creatures. How about we give them tusks so they can wound as well as tear apart?'

Linwood saw the theatre of that option immediately.

'I love it. Darn, you're good at this. I was thinking, we must give the Justice Seekers weapons too, or it'll be slaughter. If we kill too many, Fortrillium won't be happy.'

'Agreed,' said Hannah. 'But let's keep them basic to force close-up combat.'

All heads turned to see who was walking into the room. It was Damien Hunter with a woman following behind him. Hannah couldn't quite see her.

'Get that image off your console. Don't let the Law Lord see it!' she warned.

'And you remember to use only your Gridder name.'

Hannah returned to her terminal and waited for her turn to chat to the Law Lord. There was something about the tone of her voice she recognized as she made her way through the office, talking first to the Head Gridder. That voice was familiar, but she didn't want to turn around and stare.

She could sense Damien Hunter and the Law Lord making their way up to her work area. She would be next in line.

'Good morning, Janexx2. This is Law Lord Slater.'

A massive rush of adrenalin surged through Hannah's body. Lucy's mum. What should she do? They weren't supposed to acknowledge outside relationships. Did Hunter know? Was he testing her? She pretended to finish her typing to buy a delay of few seconds. How would she greet Talya?

Hannah turned to face Talya. She saw it in her eyes for a split second. Talya had apparently made the same decision. Don't let on.

'Good morning, Law Lord Slater. I'm very pleased to meet you!'

Hannah almost forgot to extend her hand to shake Talya's, which was outstretched. She was so used to not embarrassing her friends in The Climbs, she occasionally forgot how to behave on Silk Road.

Talya asked a few routine questions and moved on to the next Gridder. Hunter asked her how she was settling in, congratulated her on the excellent trial by fire, then rejoined Talya. Hannah felt Talya's eyes gesture momentarily as they parted. She wanted to get a message to her.

Hannah stood up to leave the room. She needed a moment to compose herself, and she headed to the restroom.

Her face was red when she examined herself in the mirror. Had she turned red when they were talking, or had it just happened out of relief?

Talya walked in moments later. She'd spotted her opportunity to speak.

'Hannah, we've got to be fast. I need to tell you something.

Lucy and Joe are in The Grid. They got caught doing whatever it is you were all up to. The authorities don't seem to know you're involved yet, but be careful, Hannah. They're watching us all.'

If Hannah's face had been red before, it was now

completely white. She felt her stomach tighten – the nausea was back with a vengeance. She didn't know what to say.

'Lucy and Joe are in The Grid? Oh, my God. What have I done?'

Talya put her hand on Hannah's arm. She looked as if she was about to faint. Instead, she vomited into the sink. Talya helped her to clean up.

'That's Lucy who's caught in the labyrinth, isn't it? I know it, we've trapped Lucy, haven't we?'

Hannah's eyes were red with tears, she was distraught.

'Hannah, listen to me. You've got to calm down. You need to walk out of here and go back to your desk. They mustn't know we talked, you've got to pull yourself together.

Wiz, Mitchell and I will be working on the outside. There's a WristCom in The Grid somewhere, see if you locate it and get it to them. If you can do that, I think we can do the rest.'

Hannah dried her eyes and composed herself. If she'd only known it was Joe and Lucy in there. Could she have done anything differently? They were planning to sacrifice Lucy next. She had to do something about that. How could she have been so callous?

The restroom door opened and instinctively they walked away from each other as if they'd just been passing by. It was a Centuria, hurrying things along, dispatched by Hunter no doubt. Hannah kept her head down and walked towards the door, as if she'd been doing exactly that when the door opened. She needed to make sure nobody saw she'd been crying.

Talya moved towards the sink to wash her hands. She didn't look at Hannah, but continued as if they hadn't been talking at all. The Centuria accompanied her back to

Hunter's side, then slid out of the room, back to his post, wherever that was.

'I think we're done here,' Hunter announced. 'Have you seen everything you wanted to see, Law Lord Slater?'

'Yes, thank you. It's been very helpful.'

It had been useless and completely uninformative, of course. But at last Talya had seen a shaft of light in the darkness. They had an insider. If they could get Max's help to locate the WristCom concealed in The Grid, Hannah could manoeuvre Joe and Lucy towards it. If Wiz and Mitchell were able to make some progress with their own investigations, perhaps – just perhaps – they might get them out of there alive.

As Talya exited the room with Damien Hunter, she put her hand to rest on Hannah's desk in passing, as if guiding or steadying herself. Hannah got the message, though it would not have been noticed by anybody else in the room.

Talya was telling her she wasn't on her own; they were all fighting together. But Hannah had more pressing matters on her mind. Later that evening they'd be releasing four terrible beasts into the labyrinth. The first of those creatures would be heading directly for Lucy. She had sentenced her best friend to death.

Isolation

Lucy's voice was going hoarse. She decided to stop screaming out for help. She'd been terrified when the Mode changed in The Grid. It had shaken her out of her sleep, and her head was sore and painful. Her arm was red raw.

She thought back to what had happened in the woodland. She'd woken up and seen that everybody else was asleep. Chris was still, so she decided to head out and look for food. He'd needed her reassurance, but she'd felt a bit useless. Unable to leave Chris, she'd been more passive than she would have liked. She figured that if Chris was being looked after at least he wasn't putting himself in harm's way. But she felt tied down and she wanted to contribute. Finding some food would be the most useful contribution she could make.

It was still dark when she left the camp area – there was just enough light to see where she was going. With no experience of foraging for survival on Silk Road, she didn't know where to begin, but she set off anyway. They'd eaten berries as children; there had to be berries in the woodland.

Lucy had walked towards the water first. She was anxious to freshen up and get a drink before she moved deeper into the trees. As she cupped her hands to collect water, a twig broke to her side. She stopped and looked. There was nothing there, she was certain. She continued to drink, plunging her hands in several times to quench her thirst. As she started to splash water onto her face, she became aware of a noise immediately behind her. She jumped, but was too late.

Whatever – or whoever – it was, they were fast. She felt a blow to her head before she lost consciousness and fell to the ground.

She was vaguely aware of someone – a man – talking. It was Schälen's voice. He was carrying her. She couldn't focus on what he was saying, the words just drifted in and out, she could only pick out fragments.

'You're my first trophy ... should have stayed with your friends ... where they can't find you ... hope you enjoy what I've got planned for you ...'

Lucy knew it wasn't good, but she couldn't stay conscious long enough to catch a full sentence. Then he threw her on the ground and she felt intense pain in her arm. He held his hand over her mouth so she couldn't cry out. The pain was searing, she'd never known anything like it. She passed out again, the pain was too much.

She woke with a start. The woodland was spinning around her – no, it was pixelating like something might on her console. Her hands and feet were tied, and there was something around her mouth which was making breathing difficult. Her arm was so raw. What had Schälen done to her?

She struggled as she watched The Grid change around her. The pixels moved and coloured. The dirt she was resting on became hard, cold and damp as the air quickly moved from still and fresh to sodden and heavy.

It was dark, except for the glow of a light further down the tunnel. It was a flame, some kind of torch. It felt as if she was back in the sewer again. This seemed very similar. Only this was higher and wider, and there was no water running through it.

Lucy's eyes adjusted. She was in a square, stone-built cell-like room without a door. There was a long passageway in front of her, lit by torches. There seemed to be many exits leading off that main tunnel, but the light wasn't good enough, and she couldn't really see.

Lucy rubbed the gag around her mouth against her shoulder. Gradually she loosened it and it hung limply around her neck.

She tried to shuffle her sore arm towards the light to see what wounds Schälen had inflicted upon her. It was so painful. As the light fell onto the top of her shoulder, she couldn't believe what she saw. He'd peeled a line of flesh from above her elbow to just below her shoulder joint. He'd left it hanging there. She winced to look at it.

It hurt like hell, but it was almost worse to see than it was to feel.

Out of the darkness came a bestial roar, and she shuffled into the dark corner, screaming out in fright. It was like nothing she'd ever heard before. Whatever it was, it wasn't friendly. She called out several times – the others had to be somewhere in the tunnels, but her cries just seemed to encourage the growls of whatever beast was lurking in the dark passageways. It didn't appear to be moving, so she decided to stay still and quiet.

It was difficult to make out sounds in the tunnels; she thought she'd heard voices, but they were far away and she couldn't be sure.

The rest of the group had to be in there with her. She'd become separated because of Schälen. Her first priority was to loosen her ties. If Schälen came back, it would probably be to take another slice of flesh from her. She needed to be able to fight back. Hell, her arm was sore, it was beginning to stiffen and become difficult to move.

Lucy worked away at the binding around her hands. She couldn't hear the creature anymore and there were no further echoes of voices – or whatever it was she'd heard.

She was finally beginning to loosen the knot when she heard footsteps approaching. They were slow and deliberate. It was so hard to see in that light, but she was certain. It was the silhouette of a man. It was Schälen, it was his height and build, she was sure. She watched him as he reached the torch on the wall closest to her and extinguished the flame. She was in complete darkness. The ties around her hands and feet were still too tight to shake loose. And all she could hear was the sound of approaching footsteps getting closer and closer in the darkness.

Located

In spite of being in considerable pain, Max Penner went to work as usual. He felt trapped by his circumstances and he cursed his bad luck in finding the WristCom in the first place.

If he'd just kept his head down and done his job, he wouldn't be wearing a blood-stained bandage on his hand. If he'd recovered and reported the WristCom, rather than concealing and using it, he wouldn't be in the fix he was in now.

Max was also regretting his resistance when Talya came to question him. Like most people in The City, he was aware of her from the screens. He should have known what a formidable force she'd be. It was useless standing up to her – she was used to getting what she wanted. If she already knew what he'd done to conceal the WristCom, he didn't have a choice. He'd either have to work with her or she'd report him to the Centuria. Max suspected his wounded hand was the least of his problems.

He quite liked Talya. He understood why she'd been driven to do what she'd done. Max felt as if he was usually on the side of the losers; he'd dared to imagine for a minute that, for once, he might actually get to be part of something amazing if he stuck with Talya.

However, after a lifetime in The City, most people didn't dare to hope. The grip of Damien Hunter and Fortrillium was fierce; any protests or resistance were quashed in an instant, and nothing ever seemed to change.

President Delman seemed invincible. He was an old man but was showing no signs of flagging. He had a powerful and commanding presence – it appeared he would be in charge forever.

Max sat at his desk and sighed. He'd been challenged at security about his hand. They'd even scanned it to ensure he wasn't using the dressing to conceal anything. He hated the scrutiny – the one thing nobody needed in The City was unwelcome attention. If only the Centuria had known that one of their own Law Lords had mangled his hand with a kitchen knife. He told them it had been caused by a power tool he'd been using at home. He'd had to add that it was borrowed from a friend. Somebody of Max's pay grade would not have had access to power tools otherwise.

'I should have got my friend to do the work. I didn't really know how to operate it,' he'd joked. It was difficult to tell what the reaction was from the Centuria. Those helmets hid everything. He'd been waved through and he assumed it was all over.

His new challenge was to figure out a way he could retrieve or locate the WristCom for Talya. She was hell-bent on getting it to Lucy and her friend. She was also convinced that if she could make a direct contact with the Justice Seekers they could somehow be guided to safety. Max wasn't so sure, but he'd play his part. All he wanted was to get out of this situation alive, he'd settle for that.

So Max sat and pondered his options. Only the bots could enter and leave The Grid, but he was forbidden to use them during a trial, unless there was a technical issue which had to be fixed. That had only happened twice in the time he'd been doing the job. The bots had been sent in, but he'd been supervised throughout the process. He'd had three Centuria breathing down his neck all of the time.

It had to be coordinated with the Gridders, whose job it was to close down the relevant grid sections in the gameplay area so that none of the Justice Seekers could enter them. All it took was a wall, a secured door, a precipice or some deadly hazard and nobody would ever get near to those areas while essential maintenance work was being carried out. It was a carefully coordinated situation, and under normal circumstances it presented few issues for Max.

However, it would be tough to locate the WristCom with so much Centuria attention. He dare not take the risk. It wasn't just himself he'd be exposing – it would reveal what Talya was up to as well, and they'd probably end up in The Grid together as punishment. Max didn't fancy his chances if it came to that.

He had to find an excuse to get a bot into The Grid, and it would have to be something compelling. He'd caught some of the progress of the trial on the screens that morning when he'd activated the live feed on his console.

The Justice Seekers were in some type of labyrinth, and the commentary on the screens had been very animated about what might happen there later. He could see Talya's daughter in some sort of dilemma. She'd become separated from the main group. The rest of them appeared to be contained, though one person had broken off before the Gridders had cordoned off the main party by putting a wall in their way.

It struck Max that a labyrinth would be the ideal place in which to run repairs. The Gridders had already rendered a block in the tunnels to contain the main group. In a network of passageways they'd be able to steer the Justice Seekers wherever they wanted to.

What he needed was a distraction. Whatever was happening with Talya's daughter seemed to be the primary activity at that time. It appeared to Max to be a sideline story, a subplot to the main trial. They'd save the kills for later that day, that's why the main group had been penned up. Fortrillium liked the main action to take place when the biggest audiences were available. It helped to keep the population of The City in its place.

There was a NightCam trained on Lucy. It kept flitting between Lucy and the man who was walking along the corridor, making his way to where she was being held captive. A map was being displayed on Max's screen showing where this man, Schälen, was in relation to her. They were playing the situation for tension. Every time the man got closer, they'd place a block in his way and he would have to divert through the labyrinth.

If Max could disable the camera, that would create an emergency in terms of the current trial. They'd need to send in a bot straight away, they would not want to miss whatever violent situation they had conspired to create in The Grid.

Max had no direct access to the cameras, but it might be possible for Talya to do something about that. She hadn't given any details to him, she was far too smart for that, but it had been clear from their conversation over the carving knife that she was up to something. And she would be contactable via Fortrillium's internal messaging system. He'd have to be cautious, though, he'd need to make sure the message wasn't flagged for security reasons. Then it struck him. He'd got a genuine reason to contact Talya, after her formal visit to the facility the day before. If he played things carefully, it would just look like he was responding to a query.

Max shut down the feed from the screens and started to type a message:

Class: Confidential F

Attention: Law Lord Slater

Reference: Query made during official visit to Fortrillium facility.

Response: The Grid uses a combination of fixed and

mobile cameras. The mobile cameras used are deployed via drones. They have both night-time and daylight capabilities. There are twenty mobile cameras in total and eighty fixed cameras.

Max paused at his screen. None of this would create alerts from Fortrillium, it was perfectly reasonable for him to give information to somebody of Talya's access level. He'd flag the message as an 'F-Level' secure send, there would be no problem. He'd answered a similar query from a Gridder only two weeks previously. There was no name, of course, that was encrypted and digitally authenticated, but his reply had been in exactly the same style. The Gridder had wanted to know about body cleaning and whether corpses could be removed before the trial end. As it turned out, they just had to be contained within the rendered environment. They rotted away until the bots could get in there to clean it all up.

Max continued to type:

By way of example, the camera currently filming the progress of the trial (at time 08.47) is controlled by drone CTD/a2 because there is no view available via a fixed camera in that unique environment.

The camera trained on the main group (at 08.48) is a fixed camera as the group are located on the outer perimeter of The Grid, even though the appearance on screen is that they are deep in the heart of the labyrinth.

If the cameras break down, the maintenance bots are deployed to repair as soon as possible.

I hope that answers your query.

I am sorry I was unable to clarify these details at the time of your visit, but I managed to secure this information from our technical team.

Please get in touch if you require additional information.

Max Penner

Max covered his tracks by calling the technical department and asking the same questions Talya had supposedly raised. He adjusted the timings of the camera views to make sure they were after his call. Then, for good measure, he copied in Damien Hunter so that everything appeared to be above board.

He hoped Talya would be sharp enough to understand what he'd done. Of course, she had never raised those questions during their brief meeting, but it was plausible enough.

Max sent the message, knowing it would be delivered directly to Talya's WristCom. If she was fast, they'd be losing that camera feed very soon. He had to be ready.

Before the end of the day, Max was planning to locate that WristCom and place it in the hands of Talya's daughter. If she survived that long. Then he hoped that Talya would just move on and leave him well alone.

____

CHAPTER SIX

Wired

Wiz had done what he had set out to do. It was morning at last, he was exhausted, and he was making his way back to Harry's apartment. The aerials were securely fastened to the towers. It had been an easy job once he'd got the hang of it. He just needed to check his route more carefully before he started climbing up the scaffold frames on the roofs of the tower blocks. They hadn't been in use for over a hundred years – of course they were beginning to rust through and decay.

Throughout the night, he'd been thinking about what had happened with the Centuria. It hadn't felt right to Wiz. Disaffected Centuria? It seemed unlikely to him. Leo had been very convincing, though. Why didn't they kill him there and then? That's what the Centuria usually did. It was almost strange to find real human beings underneath those helmets, there wasn't a lot of evidence to show any humanity most of the time.

Like Leo, Jody had seemed okay too, but Julia was a bit

too prickly for Wiz's taste. As he'd been speaking to Leo, he might easily have been a friend, he was so relaxed and informal. Could you be friends with the Centuria? Wiz shuddered. He'd seen them do some horrible things in his lifetime. Still, they'd left him alone to get on with the job. He'd been extra careful as he'd moved to the second and third tower blocks, making sure he wasn't being tailed. Wiz was an expert at avoiding detection, he was completely satisfied that nobody was following him.

He'd have to wait and see, as far as the Centuria were concerned, but he'd be mindful of the experience in everything he did. The WristCom would prove invaluable. Had they tapped it? Probably. But Wiz would let Mitchell take a look, he'd figure out if it was safe for him to use. A WristCom in The Climbs, though? Now that was a useful piece of equipment to have in your pocket.

Wiz had succeeded in rigging up three aerials across The Climbs. He started with the highest tower he could find, then achieved line of sight between two successively lower towers. The final tower would be directly in front of Harry's apartment window. The signals from the sewer would flow backwards and forwards and he'd be able to continue his work undetected and away from the stench of the tunnels.

He hadn't been able to work any faster. If Mitchell had been with him, perhaps the two of them could have been hacked into the networks already. Wiz checked himself – it was unfair to curse Mitchell. He wouldn't have been able to work overnight in The Climbs, he'd have to leave before Segregation. Wiz hoped he'd made his way to Harry's apartment as soon as Segregation had been lifted so they could make a start straight away.

There would be no sleep for him that day, he'd have to

keep going. As he walked towards Harry's tower block, Wiz became aware of the screens showing unusual activity for that time of day. Normally there would be news bulletin material and Fortrillium propaganda films, but there seemed to be a bit of a buzz that morning.

Wiz stopped to watch. In spite of it being early in the morning, many other residents in The Climbs were doing the same. There had been a big and unexpected change in The Grid. Wiz could see they'd switched the Modes already, and that startled him – he thought they were safe until early evening.

He was stunned to see a camera shot of Lucy in some sort of chamber. Her feet and wrists were bound, she looked terrible. Her hair was matted with blood from a wound on her forehead and there was something hanging from her arm. The camera zoomed in for the benefit of the viewers on the screens. Wiz retched as he realized what he was looking at. It was a roll of flesh hanging from Lucy's arm. The camera switched views. There was Joe. They were separated, but at least both of his friends were still alive.

Then a third camera view appeared on the screen. Wiz saw he'd have to move faster if he was going to save his friends. The commentator was getting very excited about the man making his way up the tunnel. His name was Schälen, a serial killer who'd been sentenced to trial in The Grid. Somehow he'd got a knife. It was long, sharp and had a serrated blade. He was heading for Lucy, having broken off from the main group in the labyrinth. But it was the meaning of this man's name that made Wiz shudder. The commentator took great delight in explaining that Schälen meant 'to peel'. The man heading directly for Lucy, with a knife in his hand, was going to peel her alive.

Deceptions

President Josh Delman had The Pact out on his desk. The pages were brown and fragile. Only two people in the entire city had access to this document. One was Damien Hunter, the other the President. Only, Delman's copy was slightly different from Hunter's. This edition was fully intact. Tucked into the back were the pages that had been torn from Hunter's transcript.

It was those subsequent pages that were preoccupying the President. He had read them over and over in a state of constant anxiety. There was no way he could let Hunter know what was going on. That secret would need to stay with him.

They were hours away from the Centurial. That would be when he made his final play. He was relieved that the current trial was preoccupying Hunter, that and his appointment of Talya Slater as Law Lord.

The Centurial marked the hundredth anniversary of the creation of The City. One hundred years ago, the massive concrete walls had been erected and those fortunate enough to be inside those walls got to survive.

Nobody in The City would mark the event. Delman had made sure of that with the help of Fortrillium. There were only a handful of centenarians who remembered life before the plague, but they were no risk to him, they were simply too old. All of the books were now held by Fortrillium, so there was no access to the past. Most inhabitants in The City had been born into that life, it's all they knew.

That fateful anniversary was a matter of hours away. Delman would need to be sure he was ready. Just as he'd entered The City via The Grid all those years ago, he intended to leave the same way when the Centurial began.

As he started to reread the section of The Pact marked 'Catharsis', Teanna Schaelles entered his office. She was expected, but it annoyed him when she didn't knock. Usually he'd have admonished her for that, but Teanna was important to him, he needed his allies. There were not many he felt he could trust. Now was not the time to be falling out.

'Where are we with Mitchell now?' he began. 'Any progress?'

'He's meeting with Talya Slater and Shen Li later this morning. I think we'll get a clearer idea then.'

'Do you think he's safe?'

'I think he's unreliable but easy to handle.'

'Keep him close to you. I don't want him to waver.'

Delman placed The Pact back into his secure locker. Teanna watched his every move.

'I'm more interested in Talya Slater – she made her scheduled visit to the Gridder facility this morning.'

Delman entered his code into the locker and checked to make sure it was securely shut. Teanna observed everything.

'You know that Hannah James is one of the new Gridders, don't you?'

'I don't know her personally, but surely Hunter knows there's a connection?'

'I don't think so. Hannah has a relationship with Lucy Slater, but it has been kept out of the bounds of whatever Talya's daughter was up to.'

'So he hasn't made his own connection yet?'

'I've accessed footage from the facility tour. There are three points of interest.'

Teanna touched her WristCom and there was a sound at Delman's console. He approached his desk to watch the footage Teanna had just sent. There were three clips. On the first he watched Talya Slater and Damien Hunter in conversation walking along a corridor. There was no sound, but it looked almost cordial, the body language was not entirely hostile.

In the second clip, he watched as Hannah left the main office space, followed by Talya moments later.

'What's this?' he asked.

'That's Hannah James,' Teanna replied. 'This all happened earlier this morning at Fortrillium.'

'Why is Talya Slater following her?'

'That's why Hunter can't have made the connection yet. He must know about her daughter's friendship, but he wouldn't have left them alone if he'd been worried about any subterfuge going on.'

'Interesting,' Delman remarked as he replayed the clip.

Talya had quite clearly been alert to Hannah leaving the room. She'd spotted her opportunity and taken it. It had taken Hunter quite a time to realize what had happened. He'd summoned a Centuria to move things along when he'd seen that Talya was unaccompanied. Delman moved on to the third clip. He played it twice.

'What's this?'

'Look carefully. It only lasts for a second, but there's a final contact between Hannah and Talya at the end of the tour.'

Delman played it back again, and Teanna walked up to his desk to point it out on the screen.

'There!'

'You're right. I wouldn't have spotted that.'

'They're up to something, and Hunter doesn't know it yet.'

'What's he got on Slater and Parsons, do we know?'

'I can't access that information. He's covered his tracks well. I don't even know who he's working with. As far as I can tell, he thinks it's just Parsons, Slater and Shen Li, the one they call Wiz. He has two of them in The Grid, and they're trying to locate Li. He's still in The Climbs somewhere – the Centuria have not been able to find him yet.'

'This is good, Teanna. Hunter has been careless. He hasn't connected Mitchell with Parsons and Slater yet. We need to watch Mitchell carefully – I don't want Hunter getting to him. If they capture Shen Li, they'll make the connection to Mitchell, and we need to prevent that. Mitchell will lead us to him – he's being tailed now. Don't let him know we're watching him; he has to think he's trusted. The key to managing that boy is flattery. He needs to think he's an essential part of our operation.'

Teanna nodded. She was well versed in the frailties which made humans so easy to manipulate. She'd recognized within minutes of first meeting Mitchell that he was vain and had a strong sense of self-importance. That made him an easy puppet to control.

There was an awkward silence. Teanna wanted to ask something, but she wasn't sure how it would be received. Delman sensed it. Teanna was usually forthright and confident – he knew what she was going to ask.

'What's on your mind, Teanna?'

'I was thinking about my grandfather,' she began, hesitantly.

Delman knew it would be about that, it always was. Usually a display of short temper and intolerance prevented her from asking too many questions, but over the years she'd continued to chip away, determined to excavate the truth.

'We've discussed this a thousand times, Teanna,' he responded impatiently.

That usually discouraged her from pushing at the door any further.

'It was something my father said when I was taken away. It's been troubling me for many years now.'

'Your father was a dear friend, Teanna, as was your grandfather. They were very loyal to me, and your grandfather saved my life ... I only wish I'd been able to repay the favour.'

Teanna had heard all of this before. This was a conversation they'd gone through many times. But Teanna couldn't help but think the President was withholding a crucial piece of information from her.

'Your father was furious with me for taking you. You know that.'

'Yes, but why would he warn me not to trust you? You were friends, weren't you?'

'Of course we were good friends, but he was frustrated that you had to leave Centrum. He blamed me for that – I was taking his daughter from him.'

'Do you trust me now, Teanna?'

That caught her off her guard.

'Of course I do, sir. It was just the way my father said it – it was the last thing he said to me.'

'Teanna, what can I tell you to put your mind at ease? Your father was under a lot of stress at the time; he said a lot of things to me he probably regretted. But you understand why I had to take you, Teanna, your father was too old by that time, he might not have survived until ...'

Delman cut himself short before finishing the sentence. This is how she chipped away at him, getting little snippets of information every time. He'd almost mentioned Catharsis, but she wasn't to know about that. If her father was still alive, she'd be reunited with him soon. He'd snatched his daughter from him as collateral. The Schaelles family had one more duty to perform for him before they were free.

Just like Edward Schaelles before him, Philip Schaelles was a talented CryoBiologist, trained by his father. He'd made significant advances since his own father's death, and it was the reason why Josh Delman needed to take his daughter. Teanna was a competent and formidable member of the security team at the place beyond The City called Centrum; she would serve well as his adjutant. Only, he hadn't told Teanna the whole truth. Philip Schaelles had been furious with Delman – he'd all but abducted his only daughter. He'd had no choice – he understood that Delman needed her as his guarantee. But he despised the man and resented every minute he'd spent parted from his beloved Teanna.

There was one other thing only Delman knew. Most people in The City believed he was the only person ever to have walked out of The Grid alive. It had become folklore in The City, and he was happy to leave it that way, it helped to maintain and sustain his power base. But, in fact, he'd entered The City via The Grid twice. The first time was fifty years previously when he'd been running for his life, hunted by those who reviled him. The second time had been years afterwards when he'd re-entered The City with a heavily sedated Teanna Schaelles.

At the time, she had believed there was no other choice and had opted to serve the President voluntarily. Her identity had been created in Fortrillium's data records, and as far as anybody knew she had always lived in The City, though nobody could recall having grown up with her. She became pivotal in the President's office, and nobody ever challenged her presence.

The first time Delman had entered The City he'd done

it on his own, out of necessity. The second time he'd done it, he'd had help, with another coerced ally waiting in the wings for the Centurial. When that time came, the masks would drop from the faces of those hiding in the shadows and the true threat would be revealed.

Confined

Joe felt the fury of helplessness. They were being toyed with and manipulated, he could tell. It was intentional that he had been split up from Lucy. He knew it – they were doing it to mess with their heads.

Lucy's screams had stopped. He couldn't tell where they were coming from anyway. They were in some sort of dark labyrinth. The light was minimal, and it was easy to get disoriented.

The roars continued to make their way along the tangled tunnels. They'd had long enough to understand that those sounds were just another part of the intimidation process, there to scare in readiness for the next Mode.

They'd had to accept they were not going to find Lucy. They'd set out along the gloomy, echoing passageways, trying to follow the voice. They'd make a left turn, then a right turn, walk along another tunnel, and then lose any sense of where they were or where they had been. Sometimes they would encounter doors or obstacles that blocked their way, at other times the passage would be clear.

After an hour of wandering, it had become apparent to the entire group that they were being herded. Joe was sure they were just going round in circles. It was so difficult to tell. Lucy's cries had ceased, though the growls from whatever creatures were waiting in the darkness continued to unnerve him.

Clay had finally called time on the exercise when they'd taken a number of sharp turns only to be manoeuvred to a place where they knew they'd been before. Ross had been canny enough to tear a strip off his orange overalls and leave it hanging from one of the sconces lining the tunnels. It had taken them minutes to return to the marker.

'Enough!' Clay announced. 'This Mode has not begun yet, we're wasting our energy.'

'I'm so hungry,' Chris complained. They really did need to find food soon.

'I'm not giving up on Lucy,' Joe interrupted. 'Food or no food, we can't just abandon her.'

'We're not helping her like this, Joe,' came Marjani's voice. 'We could walk around forever in here.'

Chris complained about his hunger again. He was becoming agitated and anxious; he would need to be calmed somehow.

'Joe, Lucy is our highest priority, but we can't help her if we're exhausted and unprepared when the trial begins. I don't believe they'll let her come to any harm before the trial. You know how it works – they like a big audience for the trials.'

'I agree,' said Miron. 'I know you want to help, Joe, but we've got to think ahead to the next Mode. We need to get Chris sorted out if we can.'

Joe knew they were right, but he wanted to scream out along the tunnels. He was angry and frustrated, furious with himself for not being able to come up with a plan.

'It's okay, Joe. She'll be alright.'

The unfamiliar voice came from the darkness. It was Grace. So far she'd kept silent. She looked terrified most of the time. Grace was supposed to be guilty of assault, but somehow Joe couldn't picture it.

'Are we agreed then?' asked Clay.

There was a consensus that they should wait and preserve their energy. They would need to figure out a strategy to survive in those tunnels, whatever was going to be unleashed upon them.

'You're unusually quiet, Schälen,' Ross said, as he retrieved the rag marker from the lighted torch to his side.

Everybody looked around.

'Schälen?'

'When did we last see him?' asked Clay.

'He was with us when the Mode changed. I'm sure he's been with us most of the time,' said Miron.

'I don't remember seeing him after we left the marker,' Clay picked up. 'Joe, Grace, Marjani?'

There was no response – they'd lost Schälen.

'Is he dangerous, do you think?' asked Joe, quickly becoming frantic about Lucy again.

'It's difficult to tell,' Clay tried to reassure him. 'I don't think he's here to help us, but whether or not he'd actually harm us, who knows? I'm really not sure yet.'

That didn't help to reassure Joe.

'I've got to go after him. Is anybody coming with me?'

The members of the group looked to Clay for guidance, but he said nothing.

'I'll come with you,' volunteered Ross. 'I can't say I've taken to the man.'

'Are you alright with that, Clay?' asked Joe.

Clay wasn't keen, but he nodded anyway. Joe began to walk away with Ross. There was a loud rumble. Suddenly walls came crashing down, blocking the exits all around them.

'Dammit!' cursed Joe. 'They're toying with us!'

'You need to stay calm, Joe. They're winding you up

ready for the main trial. If you use up all your energy before it begins, you'll not be able to fight when the time comes.'

Joe knew Clay was right, but it didn't stop him cursing and vowing revenge for the next few minutes. He was embarrassed to see everybody looking at him when he'd finished.

'I'm sorry,' he apologized. 'I needed to get that out of my system.'

Ross put his hand on Joe's shoulder. There were words of support from all of the other Justice Seekers.

A doorway opened behind them as suddenly as the other passageways had been closed. There was a new, dark tunnel behind them now. There was only silence; the roars of the beasts had quietened.

'I think they want us to go this way,' said Miron. Huddled together, the group made their way along the newly opened route.

There were two chambers in this new tunnel, and the group split into two, with Clay and Ross grabbing the fiery torches so they could see what was inside.

'It's food!' came a cry from Chris. 'And water!'

'We've got weapons in here,' came Joe's voice from the other room. 'Nothing useful, just knives, spears, scythes and hammers.'

'They're getting us ready for the next challenge,' said Clay. 'We need to eat and prepare. This will be the last time we get to rest and plan before it begins. We should make the most of it.'

The food was basic: bread and a selection of fruit, but the members of the group fell on it as if they hadn't eaten in days. Chris in particular seemed to be ravenous, and the others let him take more than his fair share without complaint.

Once they had fed, the conversation turned to how they were going to defend themselves. Ross held one of the hammers. It looked like a deadly implement with which to attack another human. But there was consensus that whatever they were about to face, it didn't sound human. They would have to allocate the weaponry and agree to work in defensive teams.

'They're trying to disorientate us in here,' said Clay. 'I'm guessing that's going to be a big part of what happens next.'

'I agree with Clay,' said Marjani. 'This is going to be a nasty fight.'

'We need to work as a team,' Clay continued. 'The way they keep opening and closing these passageways, we have to expect an attack from any side. We'll have to form a defensive circle. Does anybody else have a better suggestion?'

'Is it worth thinking about going on the offensive?' suggested Miron, but the idea was dismissed quickly as impractical. Nobody knew what was going to attack. Fortrillium would want a spectacle, and it might take all of them to fight what was coming.

The next task was to allocate the weapons. There was one for each of them, and two spares, which were intended for Schälen and Lucy. Joe was relieved Schälen hadn't got his hands on one of the weapons; they were primitive and threatening. The blades had serrated edges – they were clearly intended to make a mess. Each person took an implement they felt they could handle. Most of them had never held equipment like it before. Life could be rough in The Climbs, but if you stayed in your apartment during the hours of darkness, most of the time it was possible to avoid trouble. The Centuria were the greatest fear – their neighbours were the least of their problems.

Joe walked along the passageway with his spear, getting used to its weight and handling. The tunnel had remained closed off. There was nothing he could do.

Most of the others had decided to rest, on Clay's advice. But Joe was going to stay alert and awake. When the creatures came down the tunnels, he intended to do everything in his power to protect the group and fend off the attack.

Then he was going to kill the worst creature of them all. Schälen was going to feel the full force of his fury before the day was out.

CHAPTER SEVEN

Plotting

Talya gasped with frustration. She felt she needed to be in four places at once. There was just too much to do and not enough time to do it. All the time her mind was on Lucy and Joe, but there was so much else that needed to be sorted out too.

She shouted at Jena and immediately regretted it. When she'd left, Harry had been in a weak state. She was frail and elderly, it was no surprise she hadn't pulled through her ordeal. It wasn't Jena's fault, and it was unfair to blame her. She'd covered Harry's body and wrapped it in all the threadbare sheets and blankets she could find. With Dillon, they took her corpse to an empty room where they left it with as much dignity as they could. They would need to arrange for disposal, but it would not make any sense to draw attention to themselves. Harry's body would have to wait until later – they'd organize a small gathering of friends to mark her passing before her body was incinerated.

Talya recalled Harry once telling a story about how

bodies were sometimes buried, not burnt, when she was a child. Space was at a premium within The City walls, and now everybody who died was incinerated. There were no graveyards or markers; a death in The City was like a disappearance, there was no memorial left to the deceased.

Harry had told Talya how she'd like be buried – she'd always hated the idea of incineration. Could they give Harry her dying wish?

It was too much to think about, there were other lives to try to save first. Talya apologized to Jena, and she could see how the ferocity of her attack had alarmed Dillon. Wiz was already at the apartment. He'd been just as upset about Harry and had helped Jena to make sure the body would stay cool for as long as possible.

They were expecting Mitchell at any time. They desperately needed to regroup and make their plans. They were all aware of Lucy's perilous situation, and even Jena had used her time to help get them ahead. She and Dillon had fetched water supplies and moved food from their own apartment. Wiz and Mitchell would be able to make a base there and stay hidden. Who knew how long they'd go undetected?

Steps and heavy breathing were heard out in the corridor – it was Mitchell.

'What's all the blood doing on the staircase? Is everybody alright?'

Wiz told him about Harry's death. He looked unsettled. On Silk Road, death was not a regular occurrence, but in The Climbs you lived with it every day.

Talya was quick to convene the group. There would be no time for mourning until Lucy and Joe were out safely. Wiz had already managed to start configuring the equipment, and he was making the final adjustments to an aerial which was hanging out of the apartment window.

'Where are you up to, Wiz?' she began.

'It's looking good. I've managed to hop a reliable signal from the sewer, across The City via a couple of tower blocks and onto the roof of Progressive Block. I'm as sure as I can be that nobody saw me – I don't think I'd be speaking to you now if I had been seen.'

Wiz hesitated, unsure whether to mention his encounter with the Centuria. He decided to wait a while before venturing this information.

'We can now access and interrogate both data sources via the consoles in this room. You got some good kit, Mitchell. Thanks for that.'

Wiz was feeling annoyed with Mitchell's absence – he'd been left to do everything on his own overnight. But he contained his resentment, it was not the time to pick fights.

'No problem,' Mitchell replied, his cheeks colouring slightly.

'The rig looks good, Wiz. We need to take a data stream each and begin extracting some useful information.'

'I have a new job for one of you,' Talya interjected. 'Have either of you managed to speak to Hannah recently?'

There were blank looks. Only Wiz spoke.

'How did she get on in the contest? I'd forgotten all about it with everything that's going on.'

'She's at Fortrillium now, she's part of the team running this trial. She didn't realize it's Joe and Lucy in there – they don't get to see the identities or images of the Justice Seekers.'

'Can we talk to her? When is she off shift?' asked Mitchell.

'We can't talk freely to her – they're locked up in

Fortrillium until the trial ends. I took a tour around the facility earlier today. They have to maintain the integrity of the trial so the entire thing is anonymous. She was horrified when she found out what was going on.'

There was silence again – they all felt for Hannah, she was in a desperate situation.

There was a sound from Talya's WristCom. She was going to ignore it, but something compelled her to look. It was a message from Max Penner, with secure encryption.

'Wait a moment,' she said. 'I need to look at this. This is good news – I think we're in with a chance here. I've got a contact who's as close to The Grid as we can get. I'm not going to go into the details right now, but there's a WristCom in there, and there's a chance we can get to it.

Mitchell and Wiz, we need to take out a camera in The Grid. It's the one that's trained on Lucy right now.'

She tried to keep speaking but needed to take a moment. She thought of Lucy in that dark, lonely cell with Schälen making his way in her direction. She tried to focus. There was nothing they could do for Lucy unless they held firm on the track they were on.

'One of those data streams leads directly into Fortrillium. I want one of you to work on that. It has to be fast, my contact needs the camera taken out of action so he can send in the bots. If we can get to the WristCom, we can communicate with Joe and Lucy.'

'We need to figure out where the external signal is coming from too,' said Mitchell. 'At the end of this trial, someone is going to try and finish off the Justice Seekers, and we need to be ready for that.'

For a few seconds Mitchell forgot about his meeting with the President and he was back with his friends. He considered sharing what had happened but thought it better to keep it to himself. After all, nobody was in trouble, the President didn't know all of the details.

'How will we get them out, though, even if we can keep them alive?'

Everybody was surprised to hear Jena speak.

'I don't know, Jena. I think the best we can hope for is to keep them alive and find out what Matt and Tom were on to before they died.'

So many lives had been lost already, so many other lives were at risk, the challenge before them seemed too enormous.

'What are you like on consoles, Dillon? Has Joe ever taught you what he knows?'

Wiz looked at Dillon – they needed an extra pair of hands.

'I'm okay,' he replied. 'I can help if you show me what to do.'

'What about me? I want to help.'

Jena spoke again. Wiz wasn't sure he'd ever heard Joe's mum speak before. She tended to nod or shake her head. She never volunteered conversation. Joe had told him and Mitchell that it wasn't always that way. He remembered her as happy when he was a child. Before Matt was killed, that was.

'You're going to need to make sure that Mitchell, Wiz and Dillon can keep working, Jena. If I don't have to think about you all, I can get on with my own battles. You need to keep the food and water supplies coming.

I'd like you to try to find a place we can bury Harry when all of this is over. Do you think you can do that?'

Jena nodded, then replied, 'Yes, of course. There's something else I need to tell you all.'

Everybody in the room looked at her. They were seeing

a side of her they'd never seen before, except for Talya, who was beginning to recall the Jena Parsons who'd been her friend on Silk Road not so many years before.

Jena moved over to the mattress which had formed Harry's bed. She pushed her hand underneath and felt around, pulling out something dark and metallic. It was a gun.

'Where did that come from?' asked Talya, amazed at what she was looking at. 'That's Centuria issue only, nobody has those.'

'I've had it for a long time,' Jena replied, 'since just after Matt died. I vowed never to feel as defenceless as I did on that night when they took Matt away. I couldn't do anything about it then, but if they ever come into my home again, I'll kill them.'

Talya recognized that hatred – she'd felt it herself since Tom's disappearance. It seemed that Jena had been coping with things in her own way, but now this new rage would be useful.

'Where did you get that from?' asked Wiz.

'It was Matt's. We still had friends on Silk Road before they sent us to The Climbs – it was removed from the inventory of possessions after his death.'

'Do you still have that contact at Fortrillium?' asked Talya.

'No, he's dead now, the secret is safe. He died a long time ago – he was involved in a shoot-out in one of the tower blocks.'

'So who's going to take the weapon?' asked Mitchell, who was both terrified and exhilarated by this turn of events.

'It might have saved me carving up somebody's hand if I'd had that,' said Talya. 'A decent weapon can be a useful thing to have. There's no way I'll get that through security; it needs to stay this side of the wall.

Keep it here for now, Jena. You never know when you might need it. I hope you will never need it,' she added, but Talya thought it unlikely the weapon would get through events unfired.

'What about you?' asked Jena. 'What's your plan?'

'I've been summoned as Law Lord to be at the beginning of the next Mode this evening. I've got to be there for 20:00 hours, that's why I'm hoping nothing much will change until then. We have just a couple of hours to move things on, so we need to get that WristCom to Joe and Lucy today if we can. Hannah will do what she can to help at her end, though I'm not sure what she can manage from Fortrillium – she has people breathing down her neck all the time.'

'I need to tell you something,' Wiz began. He seemed hesitant. 'I have a WristCom. You can communicate with me now if Mitchell can set up a secure channel.'

'You people are full of surprises!' said Mitchell. 'Where did that come from?'

Wiz decided to stay quiet about his new Centuria contacts, he wasn't sure what to make of it still. He thought that the less Talya knew the better, it might compromise her later.

'Like Jena, I have my contacts,' he smiled, hoping that would deflect the question. Nobody challenged any further, but it was clear he was hiding something.

'Okay, let's get to it!' said Talya. 'I'm back to Silk Road, let me know when we have a secure channel for the Wrist-Coms. The less I'm over in The Climbs, the better.'

It felt good to be doing something. They were making progress, things were moving on.

If they'd known that at that very moment Lucy was

fighting for her life to fend off a killer, the mood of optimism might have not been so intense.

Scent

Damien Hunter was glued to the screen feed on his console. He hoped Talya Slater was looking at the same images as he was – it was pure entertainment. He had to hand it to the Gridders, this trial was shaping up to be a strong one.

He'd been disappointed when there were only three Modes, as he'd hoped to draw things out a little longer. But his idea to throw Schälen into the mix at the last moment had been inspired. It was even better that the Gridders were using him so well; it had been an excellent move isolating Lucy, then allowing Schälen to break off from the primary group.

Not only would the Justice Seekers be angry, frustrated, tired and vengeful by the time the main action started, but their judgement would be diminished too. That meant more kills.

There was still Ascension to come at the end of the trial when the survivors would be slaughtered anyway, but this would be a spectacle everybody remembered.

He'd softened when speaking to Talya in the corridor. She'd been his enemy for so long, he'd almost forgotten to think of her as a human being. Damien thought of his own family – he had to save them at any cost. Nobody's children mattered more than his own, and if Talya Slater had to suffer more for him to reach his goal, then so be it.

The Centurial was almost upon them, and whatever Delman was up to he'd be forced to make his move then. The data extracted via the equipment confiscated from

Parsons and Slater was due at any time. He'd have a better idea what move to make next when that arrived.

Hunter chuckled to himself as he watched Schälen becoming more and more frustrated on the screen. He only had to walk up a long passageway to get to Lucy, but whenever he stepped forward a wall would crash down in front of him and he'd be diverted around the labyrinth. To move forward, the Gridders were forcing him to take a detour every time. He could see Lucy – he was so close – but they wouldn't let him get to her.

Lucy was struggling to get free of her restraints – Schälen had had to improvise with those. She was tantalizingly close, and Damien could only imagine how gripping this was for everybody else watching on the screens.

He'd been clear in his directives to the Gridders, though. However it ended for Parsons and Slater, it had to be slow, dramatic and painful. He needed to send out a strong message: traitors would not be tolerated under his rule. Parsons and Slater had conspired against The City. They would answer with their lives.

He was distracted by an incoming message on his console. Reluctantly he clicked away from the feed just as Schälen had been frustrated once again in the tunnels of the labyrinth. He'd tried to run at Lucy, but his route had been blocked – once again – and he was now in a thunderous rage.

The message was at the highest level of encryption. Hunter authenticated with DNA and the message opened. It was the full analysis from the activities in the sewers.

He could see that Fortrillium security had been breached. They'd been looking for Matt Parsons' files, and it appeared they'd found them too. That might have caused problems later, but it confirmed to Damien that he was right to send Joe and Lucy to The Grid: whatever they'd found out had to die with them.

He sent off a memo to get Matt's legacy storage area re-encrypted to prevent any further attempts to access it. With Parsons and Slater out of the way, he hoped the problem was contained.

It was the second set of data that was far more interesting to him, this was entirely new. If he was correct, this would get him closer to whatever Delman was up to, and it couldn't have come at a better time. With the Centurial almost upon them, he felt sure it would all come to a head very soon. He had to be ready to move fast, to save his family and get away from whatever was coming.

The data confirmed what he'd suspected for some time. The President was in contact with somebody – or something – beyond the walls of The City. They were not alone. He'd always felt it to be unlikely.

This was proof that there was more than Fortrillium, and it was a secret Delman didn't want to share. Why would he keep that to himself? Hunter felt sure it had to do with the rumours of him walking out of The Grid – that was the link, but he couldn't figure out what it all meant.

Damien sent off a second message, this time authorizing 24/7 monitoring of the second feed. He wanted to know the minute there was new activity. If Delman spoke to somebody beyond The City's walls, he needed to be the first to know.

He could feel his family getting closer, and he imagined what it would feel like to hear their voices again, to laugh and chatter as they had done before. He yearned for the return of his wife and children, it was all he could think of. He wanted to feel human again.

Damien cursed President Delman and all he'd done to

make him suffer. But he'd have his revenge on the President. He could taste the blood on his lips now. When the Centurial came, whatever it was, Hunter would be ready. He would kill his rival and rescue his family, then The City would be his alone to rule.

Arrest

Julia Levett had more to lose than her friends Leo and Jody. She was typical of the people recruited to the Centuria. She had family and connections – Fortrillium could intimidate her at any time.

She'd frequently wondered if it had been the right decision to throw her lot in with the resistance movement. It had happened slowly, though; she'd had to decide on the spur of the moment and she'd opted to save her friends.

There wasn't much Fortrillium missed, and she was amazed they'd managed to achieve so much without detection. However, with the security credentials to pass freely between Silk Road and The Climbs, Centuria were in the perfect position to assist the resistance.

Everybody hated life in The City – they were all flies trapped in the spider's web. The only difference for those on Silk Road was that they got housed and fed. They were all guilty of inaction, the will to fight had been knocked out of them years ago. She was too young to know when city residents had given up, but she figured there must have been a point at which Fortrillium had finally beaten them into submission.

She'd felt as if she could make a difference in the Centuria. Naturally athletic and active, she'd been recruited early. She knew what they were capable of, she'd grown up seeing it all around her. Less so on Silk Road, of course, and she was shocked by the horrors she'd encountered the first time she stepped into The Grid.

It was Hunter who'd turned her towards the resistance. She'd been on shift with Leo and Jody when he'd gone on one of his shooting sprees in The Climbs. She'd been a raw recruit at the time, new to that side of the wall.

Hunter had ordered them to finish off the wounded he had maimed and incapacitated, leaving the Centuria to make sure there was nobody left to bear witness. It had been all Julia could do not to throw up. She fought to contain her horror until Hunter had left the scene.

Their Quad Team leader was a man called Santo and he commanded them to finish off the wounded. Julia hadn't known what to do. She wanted to scream and run. Leo had walked over to where Hunter had discarded his weapon on the ground. Casually he picked it up and shot Santo in the head.

'You need to make a choice, Levett,' he'd said, calm and in control.

'Either you cover for us or you hand us in. If you cover for us, we can maybe save some lives and make a difference out here.'

She'd been in shock, but Julia had no other choice. There was no way she could slaughter the shot residents bleeding out and crying with pain on the road in front of her.

It was a decision she'd made in the moment. Only, when she'd thrown in her lot with Leo and Jody she'd never thought about the danger it would consistently place her in.

Julia confirmed Leo's story that one of the wounded had grabbed the discarded weapon and shot Santo before they could do anything to stop it. They'd cleared up Hunter's mess alright, but the seven badly hurt residents had been taken to a safe place where they could be given medical attention. Generally, they'd just 'disappear', relocated around The Climbs in out-of-the-way locations where the rats would get to them. Julia didn't know where they'd been taken, since Leo and Jody had kept her out of direct contact with the resistance. But three out of seven of the wounded had been saved. They'd helped three people live that day, and she knew it was her only choice.

Julia had never felt part of the team, even though she was in collusion with Leo and Jody and had covered their backs more than once in the past. There was an unspoken understanding: she was just too vulnerable. If she knew too much, Fortrillium could get to her through her family.

When a Fortrillium operative had noticed Wiz's bag in the video update Jody had filed from the top of Pegasus tower block, he'd called in his senior supervisor to take a look. Closer scrutiny had revealed there to be Fortrillium equipment in the bag, some of which was apparently live and activated.

Not long after Leo, Jody and Julia came off shift that night, Julia was detained by an armed group of Centuria, people who were supposed to be her colleagues. They beat her continuously right there on the street, demanding to know where Leo and Jody were.

She didn't know, they'd gone off somewhere into The Climbs, she never asked where they went after their shifts.

It didn't very much matter. That would be the last shift Leo and Jody would ever complete as Centuria. However, it was not the final time they would raise their weapons. Word soon reached them about Julia's arrest. They had to go to ground, the game was up. Their hands had been forced by a stupid error. The fightback would have to begin, there was no more putting it off.

Attacked

Lucy was frantic. She'd been trapped for so long, with Schälen getting closer and closer. She could hear his curses; he was screaming what he intended to do to her when he reached her, but each time he was blocked and frustrated in his efforts.

There was only so long they could keep him away from her. He was almost there now – it might have been better for her if he hadn't been goaded and angered so much.

His threats had increased in their violence, from peeling the rest of the skin from her arms to flaying her alive. She wasn't going to sit still and wait for it to come. She was working hard at the knots in her ties, and they were loosening by the minute.

The final barrier had been placed in front of her prison area at the end of the tunnel. He had to be so close. Lucy struggled and twisted, but she couldn't make any progress with the ties. Her arm was sore and stiff, the struggling hadn't helped, and the loose skin was beginning to make her feel ill.

Then there was a sound behind her. She'd expected Schälen to come from in front of her when he finally broke through, but with no warning a doorway opened behind her and he was there.

Lucy shuffled across the floor to get away. There was a flaming torch behind him, and the blade he was carrying caught the light as he got closer.

He was calmer now, and that made him even more frightening. He moved closer to her, one step at a time. When it came to intimidating his victims, he was in comfortable territory – he knew exactly what to do.

However angry he was, his shouting had stopped now.

He was deliberate, silent and slow, a predator waiting in the shadows to take its prey.

Lucy backed away, scraping the skin on her legs and arms as she did so. She screamed at Schälen, hoping that somehow her friends would hear her, but the only sounds in the tunnels came from her.

When Lucy had retreated as far as she could go, she was caught in the corner, there was nowhere else to retreat to. Schälen took one slow step at a time until she was fully in his shadow. All she could hear was his breathing. He was excited now, this was fun to him.

He crouched down in front of her. Lucy tried to kick out at him, but with sudden and crushing power he slammed his fist on her calf muscle and she immediately flinched with the pain.

'Shh!' he hushed quietly, 'The more you struggle, the more it hurts.'

Lucy didn't know what to do. If she fought him off, he became more violent. If she didn't fight him off, what might he do? She'd already had a taste of his work and didn't want to sample any more. There was only one thing for it – to fight.

Schälen moved his face close to hers, and she could feel his stinking breath. He moved the blade up to her cheek, pressing it gently into the flesh. She felt it glide through the skin, as he held it there, just below the surface. She sensed the blood begin to ooze from the wound. He smiled at her.

All the time Lucy was watching him, her eyes fixed on his. He was looking for fear, but all he saw was defiance. It urged him on. He needed to see fear, Schälen fed off terror. He moved the knife along her cheek slowly, and she felt it cutting deeper. It was hard not to recoil, but she held his gaze, looking for her moment to act.

He pulled the knife away from her cheek, then held it in front of her, as if deciding where to place it next. Still Lucy held his gaze. She didn't blink.

Schälen moved the knife to just below her ear, running it gently down her neck so it drew blood but did not cut too deep. Still Lucy stared him out, refusing to show terror or fear. He removed the knife and held it in front of her once again.

Slowly, he moved it down to the arm he'd already savaged. Inside her head, she screamed 'No!', but to his face, she remained steady.

He inserted the knife at the bottom of the flayed area, and slid it gently into the skin. Then she saw it. It was a glint in his eye, he'd been the first to flinch in their staring contest.

With all the force she could muster, Lucy kicked out wildly, pushing through the pain where he'd struck her moments before. It had taken him completely unawares, Schälen was more accustomed to having his victims in the grip of his power. He stumbled, falling backwards and instinctively putting out his hand to break the fall.

Lucy moved her bound hands and pulled the knife out of the flesh of her arm. She cut the ties around her feet and stood up. She'd been tied up too long, her legs were cramped and she struggled to start running. Schälen had recovered from his short fall, and was standing up, heading directly for her.

Lucy's feet were now free, and she might have made it if she'd been able to run straight away. Schälen lunged at her, winding her as she crashed to the floor. She dropped the knife and it slid across the floor behind them both.

She needed to free her hands. She couldn't run if they were still bound, he'd catch up with her. Lucy moved towards the knife, struggling to catch her breath, but he went to block her. She was tiring quickly. She'd had nothing to eat or drink for some time, and she knew she wouldn't be able to keep it up for long.

Schälen turned his back to her so he could take the initiative and recapture the weapon. Lucy knew she'd have to strike hard or become his captive once again. She'd seen what his intentions were and she wasn't going to stick around.

'Joe!' she called, summoning everything she could to make it sound as if her friends had come to save her. It wasn't difficult, she'd have given anything to see a friendly face at that moment.

Schälen turned to see if it was true, and he immediately saw he'd been fooled. But it was enough time to let Lucy throw herself towards the knife. She picked it up with her right hand, twisted it around so she could cut the binding and it sliced straight through, absorbing her own blood from the blade as it did so.

Lucy was free. As Schälen raised his fist to crash it into her skull, she darted down and plunged the knife into his leg. He let out a scream and his arm moved to his wound, moments before hitting Lucy's chin. She rolled away just as the doorway to her small chamber began to close.

She hadn't rolled far enough to clear it, and the barrier was about to come down on her leg. She went to draw it in, but Schälen had his hand on her foot, she couldn't move it. The barrier was inches from her ankle, she kicked one more time and managed to pull her foot in just far enough to avoid the crash. Schälen was not so lucky. Lucy heard the crunching of bones as his hand was caught by the barrier.

The small gap closed to nothing, and the last thing she

heard was the agonized cries of Schälen as his hand was crushed to a pulp by the heavy wooden doorway.

She was safe from Schälen in a long, dimly lit passageway. She called for help, but there was no reply. She tried again, just an echo.

Lucy decided she needed to get away from where the doorway had closed up. She'd seen enough of the labyrinth to know that Schälen might reappear at any time. He wouldn't make a meal of her death. After what she'd just done to him, he'd kill her straight away next time they met – if he survived the blood loss from his injury.

Lucy moved up the passageway, ducking in the doorways, but trying to keep heading away from where her fight with Schälen had taken place. Eventually, when she was sure she'd moved far enough, she took refuge in the dark corner of a side chamber and sat down.

She wiped the blood from her cheek and neck, though she could feel it was already beginning to congeal. Schälen had torn her first sleeve when he'd first cut into her arm in the wooded area, and she decided to remove the other sleeve to give her some way to clean up her wounds. The blood stains showed up clearly on the green linen of her Fortrillium overalls. She hoped her wounds weren't as bad as they looked.

For the first time that day, Lucy began to relax a little, relieved she was finally out of Schälen's grip. But she'd been distracted, she'd lost track of time. This was the second Mode, the trial proper would begin soon.

Lucy was beginning to understand why some Justice Seekers appeared to give up when she'd watched on the screens. She was only an occasional viewer, but it was difficult not to see the trials, they were screened everywhere, at all times of day.

She was tired, weak and hungry, and she wasn't sure how much fight she had left in her. If only she could reach Joe and the others – they had to be in the tunnels somewhere. They wouldn't be separated off until the final challenge, Ascension, when there were only a few survivors left. Joe had to be around somewhere.

Lucy struggled to her feet and made her way back into the main passageway. She'd lost her bearings completely, and she didn't know if she was heading closer to Schälen or further away.

Every few steps she would stop and listen. The echoes were deceptive, she was becoming scared of her own shadow. Lucy was convinced she was alone and that Schälen was nowhere near her.

As she made her way quietly up the passageway, she saw something hanging from one of the sconces up ahead. She moved faster towards the flaming torch, sure that it was a clue.

As she drew near, she could see what it was. It was a rag from orange overalls. Grace or Ross must have left it as a marker or a signal. Maybe they were looking for her? Lucy felt a massive sense of release. Her friends had to be close, they must have left the rag as a sign for her.

She called out along the tunnel several times, careless now as to whether Schälen heard her or not. She felt stronger and more positive. All she wanted was to be reunited with the group and see Joe again.

There was no reply and no sign of Schälen either. It was frustrating, she'd caught a glimpse of them, but they were nowhere to be found.

Lucy sat down once again beneath the hanging rag. It made sense to stay there – if they'd left the orange strip as a signal, she hoped they'd soon return there. She was stiff and sore, and her facial wounds were beginning to throb.

She dropped her head and closed her eyes, fighting the urge to sleep. She lost the battle. Lucy was so exhausted, she drifted off into a slumber.

She didn't know how long it was, but she woke with a start. She listened: no footsteps, no voices. What was it that she could hear? A low growl, deep and penetrating, rumbling along the dim tunnels of the labyrinth.

Cautiously she stood up, scanning for the direction of the sound. It was breathing, she was certain, but what could make a noise that deep and loud?

Quietly she made her way along the corridor. It sounded as if that was where it was coming from. She looked through a doorway to her left, and there it was:

two long tusks, jaws lined with razor-sharp teeth and eyes that shone blue in the darkness of the tunnels.

As Lucy turned to run, the beast stirred. It had smelled human blood.

CHAPTER EIGHT

Collaboration

Hannah had got Talya's message loud and clear, even though they'd barely had any time to communicate. She was still reeling from the discovery that two of the most important people in her life were trapped in The Grid. She might have killed them. On her screens, they were just identified as 001Green and 002Green. But that was Joe and Lucy, she knew it now. So who had she killed when The Justice Trial began? She'd selected that person on the crutches because they had a high affinity score to 001Green – or Joe – in particular.

Hannah wanted to curl up on the floor and cry. They'd started this scheme to infiltrate Fortrillium, with no real idea of where it would lead. What did they think? That they could just walk in and everything would be fine?

She felt as if she'd taken on more than she could cope with, but she was trapped now, there was only one way to move. Forwards.

Hannah had sat at her console for some time thinking

about the consequences of what they'd done. They were dealing with life and death, and she wished to God she'd thought it through more carefully. But this was about Joe and Lucy. She'd been around when they both lost their fathers, and she remembered the devastating consequences it had had on their lives. In spite of the danger that they were in, she knew they had to keep moving ahead, but there was no hiding from the sheer terror of her predicament.

How much could she trust Linwood? Was he for real? She'd have to test him and find out. He was about to unleash four beasts into the labyrinth, and those beasts could kill her friends. She had to try and keep them alive, she had to work with Talya to help them survive.

There was no choice but to team up with Linwood. This was his challenge. He'd asked her to help, but she'd need to do what she could to protect Joe and Lucy. They'd have to make it look convincing – the action on the screens would need to keep the engagement levels high or else Damien Hunter would be back in the office, and it wouldn't be a social call.

Hannah messaged Linwood directly to his console. It was easier if he came to her workstation, since as the new Gridder she was located away from the main cluster. He made it look as if he was passing her desk casually. At least he knew how to avoid looking suspicious.

'You've been crying. Don't let anybody see that. What's up?'

Hannah was annoyed with herself. She thought she'd managed to conceal what had been going on.

'Don't worry, I can only tell because I'm up close, nobody else will notice from over there.'

'I need to know if I can trust you, Linwood?'

There was no point dragging things out, she needed to

move fast. He looked at her, wondering what this was leading to.

'You can,' he replied. 'Definitely. What happened during Law Lord Slater's tour?'

'This is serious, Linwood. I have to know if you're a friend.'

'Look, I only became a Gridder because my brother went missing and I thought it would help me to find out where he was. I'm not tough, I'm not clever, but I could play games. I got in the only way I know how, and now I'm here I'm no further forward and I'm stuck killing innocent people. Does that help to build some trust?'

'It'll do for starters, but we could lose our lives over what I'm about to tell you. Are you ready for that?'

'Hannah, I could lose my life if I don't do a good job of this next Mode. I've been living with that fear ever since I came in here.

Seriously, whatever you've got to say probably won't surprise me.'

The Head Gridder walked by and checked in on the progress of the next Mode. Linwood was sharp, he made out that's what they were discussing at that very moment. The Head Gridder listened to what was planned, then moved on. They continued their conversation.

'I've got two friends in there. Talya Slater is the mother of my best friend.'

Linwood hadn't been ready for that, and he was stunned by this information. But he immediately caught its gravity.

'Hell, have we hurt them?'

'Not yet, but one of them is 002Green. We've let her be stalked by the weirdo.'

'Let me check up on that.'

Linwood leaned over and monitored the progress in The Grid via Hannah's console. He logged into his admin area and ran several lines of code at great speed.

'Okay, I've built in a loop for now. Every time he gets near her, his route will be blocked and he'll be diverted. Based on his Psych-Eval that's going to make him even madder, but he can't reach her for now. It'll look great on the screens and it'll keep your friend safe.'

'But what about the beasts? Nobody is going to stand a chance in there when we unleash them.'

'There's not a lot we can do when we let them loose, other than to control the exits in the labyrinth to give some protection. We have to kill off more of the Justice Seekers in this Mode. If we don't it'll be obvious. If we end up in The Grid with them, we're no help at all. You know the game here, Hannah. We have to make kills.'

Hannah was certainly beginning to understand the game a lot better. There was no choice but to kill in The Grid. The best she could hope for was to keep her friends alive a little longer, in the hope that Talya could do something from the outside. It all seemed unlikely to Hannah.

She watched the pixelated images of Lucy and Schälen on the main screen. One of those images was her friend and she'd been making plans to kill her. Now she had to keep her alive at any cost. Without being discovered.

'What can we do?'

'Here's the plan,' he began. 'We don't have a lot of options. We need to give them weapons before the challenge. I'd intended to give them only four weapons, but let's give them all a fighting chance – they can have one weapon each, maybe we can throw in a few extras too. We'll need to make your friend look good when she fights the weirdo, but we can help her get away. How strong is she?'

Hannah looked at him doubtfully. Lucy was strong, but was she any match for the serial killer? She wasn't so sure.

'We'll need to help her however we can, she's certainly very determined.'

'Okay, that's good. The best we can do for her is to herd her towards the others for protection, we mustn't leave her isolated. But, Hannah, it has to look good. If any of the others sense we're protecting people, we'll get an intervention. We have to keep the gameplay fast and interesting. Hunter will not accept low engagement levels.'

For the remainder of the day, Hannah and Linwood worked at the next Mode, assisted by the other Gridders in the team. There was a general consensus that the labyrinth was a great concept and unleashing four massive creatures into the tunnels would create a compelling and frightening gameplay scenario.

Later that afternoon, Linwood saw his chance to protect Lucy. It was he who opened up the passageway to allow her to escape. Then, in a dramatic moment which had caught the attention of everybody watching the screens, he crashed the barrier down onto Schälen's hand in full camera view. His hand was crushed, he was in considerable pain and he was bleeding profusely.

Lucy had got away – for now – and he'd made it look good. He'd steered Lucy towards Ross's orange marker; he'd placed her where she could easily be reunited with the main group.

But however much he and Hannah tried to control the action in The Grid, there was very little they could do to influence the actions of the individual Justice Seekers other than gently guide the action. They had free will, after all.

Hannah and Linwood worked steadily towards the beginning of the next Mode, as confident as they could be they'd given Joe and Lucy every chance to survive the next horrific challenge. But there were two things happening that were completely out of their control. Both of these would steer events in a direction over which they had no influence.

First, in a blood-soaked dungeon deep within the labyrinth, Schälen considered his options. His hand was almost severed, it was no use to him. But he had the resources available to help him get out of the situation. With his remaining hand, he stretched out to retrieve the discarded ties left behind by Lucy.

As he reached out, he felt the crushed bones in his hand breaking off and the skin tearing. He nearly passed out with the pain, but he'd seen his share of human agony before. He knew he was a long way off dead – the human body could endure far more than he'd been subjected to.

Slowly and deliberately, Schälen retrieved the ties, looped them below the joint in his arm and tied them as tightly as he could.

Once he'd arrested the blood flow, he began to stretch his body as far as he could to retrieve his knife. Lucy had dropped it in her rush to escape him. He strained his tethered arm and his legs to reach the knife. Schälen shouted out as another broken bone in his hand shattered with the pressure, but that last push had allowed him to flick the knife towards his free hand. He worked through the pain, pushing it to the back of his mind as he finally clasped the knife.

He was going to remove his crushed hand. There was much more pain still to endure, but he knew it was his only chance of survival. The hand would have to be cut off, bone by crushed bone, and sinew by sinew.

There was a good chance he'd pass out during the

process, but it had to be done, it was his only way out of the labyrinth. Once free, he was going after Lucy. Whatever creatures had been roaring in the tunnels earlier that day, there was only one animal she had to fear. If he caught her, he would finish her.

But there was something even Schälen didn't know about the events that were to follow. Unknown to any of the Gridders, an anomaly had been detected in the gameplay algorithms. Somebody was cheating the system, and the interferences were coming from the consoles of Janexx2 and 97TRaider. Not even the Head Gridder had access to this algorithm. It had been placed remotely onto all of the consoles to detect abnormal interference in favour of particular players.

As Reevil96 sifted through the data a second time to confirm those suspicions, it became clear that Hannah James was definitely not who she appeared to be. Whatever she was up to with 97TRaider, they were trying to protect someone inside The Grid. It would require an intervention much sooner than anticipated.

Reevil96 accessed the accounts of Janexx2 and 97TRaider via a remote and secure connection. There would be no legacy trail to detect that he'd ever been there. A few lines of code would fix things, it would redress the balance after their previous interferences.

When the four beasts were unleashed later that day, they would be hunting for two individuals now. As they scoured the tunnels of the labyrinth, seeking human blood, they would be targeted on individuals wearing a particular colour of overalls. That colour would be green, the same as the overalls worn by Joe and Lucy.

Matrix

Wiz, Mitchell and Dillon worked at the new rig for several hours, always with one eye on the screen feed, which they'd set up in view of everybody.

They'd had to place the consoles next to the windows, as they needed as much light as possible for a solar charge. Wiz was fearful they might lose power before the night was out.

'Is there nothing we can do to lay our hands on a portable power supply?' he'd challenged Mitchell.

'I could get one on Silk Road, but how will I get past security? It's too big for a bag.'

Reluctantly, Wiz had agreed. Then Dillon had volunteered an idea – it seemed to be a good one.

'How about I steal one?'

Both Wiz and Mitchell had been surprised at this. They'd never really taken that much notice of Dillon, he seemed too young to them.

'What do you have in mind?' said Wiz.

'The Centuria have power packs placed all over The Climbs. Why don't I steal one?'

Wiz and Mitchell were doubtful. They didn't want to get Joe's brother killed or thrown into The Grid beside him.

'I'll go with Jena,' he continued. 'She has a weapon. We can sort out the power supply together.'

It seemed like a good idea. Mitchell didn't want to admit it, but Dillon was slowing him down. He was quick to catch on, but his tech skills were nowhere up to their level.

'Okay, go for it!' he said, looking towards Wiz for approval. 'I'm out of here at Segregation. If the power fails on you overnight, Wiz, you'll leave Joe and Lucy very exposed in there.'

Wiz was reluctant but saw the sense of it.

'Okay, Dillon, but only with your mum – and if she takes the weapon.'

Jena had left the apartment to see what could be done about Harry's burial and pick up Joe's rounds delivering food and water. Dillon would catch her on the stairways. They gave him the signal to be on his way.

'I've got the WristCom sorted, Wiz. You can use this in relative safety now. There's a direct line to Talya and me. It's encrypted and you'll be able to communicate with us on Silk Road. The signal won't be strong, so it may not work all of the time. Send text messages if you can't reach us, they'll get delivered when you're in range again.'

Wiz nodded and continued typing at his console.

'They've scrambled the encryption on Matt's files again. I'm running multiple configurations across it, it'll break eventually.'

Mitchell leaned over to look at the code arrays sweeping across Wiz's console. He nodded. Wiz had set it up correctly, it would just be a matter of time.

They agreed to focus on accessing the cameras as Talya had requested. It would take all of their joint expertise to do that.

Wiz still wanted to clean up the audio of Delman he'd saved earlier in the sewers. Mitchell was desperate to focus on the live feed – they'd need to be able to access that directly if Delman used it again.

The two worked silently, side by side, running lines of code and trying as many permutations as they could find.

As the light began to fade during the afternoon, Wiz moved the solar charger to capture as much daylight as there was left to squeeze out of the day. Where were Dillon and Jena with the charging panel? If they could lay their hands on one of those, everything would be good.

Both were mindful of the screens feed in front of them. They'd been asked to disable the camera that was trained on Lucy, but they'd watched in horror as events in the labyrinth had played out and it had become the serial killer who was trapped in the chamber.

They'd agreed to make for the same camera still – CTD/a2 – as Talya's contact had suggested. Wiz's frustration was beginning to get the better of him. The combination of dead ends on Fortrillium's network and the scenes playing out on their screen feed made him feel useless.

It was only when the new encryption key for Matt's files was unlocked that they made the breakthrough they needed.

Mitchell was beginning to wonder if he'd made the right choice to confide in Delman. He was enjoying this work tremendously. It was really testing his tech skills; it was illegal but incredibly stimulating for someone like him. He considered his conversation with the President. He was there to report back. There was no threat yet to his friends and he was still able to continue his work. He kept his mouth shut and carried on.

Once they'd got to Matt's files once again, it was easy for them to re-route elsewhere onto Fortrillium's system. Working quickly and efficiently together, Mitchell and Wiz soon managed to access the camera array within The Grid.

'We can't get direct access,' said Mitchell. 'There's a massive firewall protecting everything, and it'll take years to break through that.'

'We don't need to penetrate the firewall,' Wiz replied. 'We just have to block the wireless feed from CTD/a2.'

'You're right!'

Mitchell was excited now. He typed at his consoles, moving between multiple screens.

'I've re-routed round Fortrillium's system. It'll go via several employees' logins. It's going to cause quite a stir.'

They watched the screen feed. It turned their stomachs. The action was entirely focused on Schälen who was sawing away at his hand with a knife.

Every now and then the screen view would flick to the main group, resting and getting used to the weaponry, to Lucy, alone in the tunnel, and then back to Schälen.

'This is going to make all hell break loose,' said Mitchell. 'It'll switch off in a moment.'

They watched as Schälen forced the knife through a shattered bone, then appeared to pass out with the pain. Wiz had to look away, but as he did so the screen went blank.

'Did we lose power?'

'It's fine, we've disabled the camera,' Mitchell reassured him.

'I'll get a message to Talya, she needs to know this.'

Wiz used his new WristCom. It worked as Mitchell had said it would, and she got straight back to him, confirming she'd alert her contact. Wiz had begun to think better of having cursed Mitchell when he was on his own in the sewer, or fighting for his life as he dangled from the scaffolding at the top of the tower block. His friend's skills were remarkable, and they'd be lost without him.

'What do we do now?' he asked.

'We just wait. Talya's contact will try to get the WristCom where Joe and Lucy can find it.'

'Okay, I'm going to clean up this audio of Delman I saved earlier. Before you go, can you work on the live feed?'

'I've got just over two hours, then I'll have to go back.'

They could have done without Segregation, but it was important that Mitchell didn't get caught out in The Climbs as Lucy had done. He would have to head back home before 20:00 hours. Besides, he had another appointment with the President and he wasn't going to be late for that.

The screens did not return to Schälen for some time, and the commentator had to switch back to Lucy and the main group as his focus. It was clear he was frustrated by not being able to watch Schälen. He made the excuse that the serial killer had passed out with pain and there was little to see at that moment. Wiz and Mitchell knew better. They just hoped Talya's contact would do what he said he would do.

There was more silent work as they tapped away at their consoles. An hour in, the camera came back on. Schälen was back, hacking at his hand.

'How long does it take to cut through a hand?' Wiz wondered. The whole process was excruciating to watch.

Mitchell got his breakthrough before Wiz. The audio feed had been bad, and he wondered if it was worth the trouble. Matt's files might hold more information now he'd managed to unlock them.

'I'm in!' he exclaimed. 'Take a look at this, Wiz. I can tell by the degradation of the feed that these signals are coming from quite a way outside The City's walls. There has to be something else out there, Wiz, or somebody, but who? Delman must know something. I'm as sure as I can be that it's his voice I heard. There's nothing coming on the feed right now, it's audio only. There's no data as far as I can tell, but that might change. We're ready when it starts up again, though. You'll be able to monitor whatever is going on.'

Wiz felt frustrated by his own tech skills once again.

Mitchell had made a great breakthrough, but his own progress had been less than impressive.

'I might give up on the audio, Wiz. You'll catch whatever they're talking about next time they communicate.'

'You've not got long left now. Can you take a look at Matt's files before you go – see if you can find anything interesting?'

'Sure, no trouble,' replied Mitchell. 'I wish Dillon would get back with those chargers, we're losing light now.'

He was right. The light was fading and it would soon be time for Segregation. It wasn't long until Mitchell stood up and announced he'd have to be on his way. Wiz thought he still had plenty of time, but he seemed anxious to leave. Mitchell wasn't accustomed to being in The Climbs after dusk, and Wiz cut him some slack – perhaps he was just scared.

'I'm on my WristCom if you need me, Wiz. I don't know how long the power will hold out, but it should get you through most of the night. Good luck!'

Wiz was left in the apartment on his own, surrounded by lashed-up screens and tech. It was serving them well, and he'd know about it the minute there was any activity on the external feed.

He decided to give the audio snippet a little more time before he moved to Matt's files. With Mitchell gone, he found it easier to think clearly. He'd been careless, he'd forgotten to try a basic audio protocol. Mitchell made him doubt his own abilities whenever he was around; he needed to become less intimidated by people who lived on Silk Road.

He'd got it. He cursed himself: fancy missing something so basic. Wiz ran the audio through a few filters, cleaned up the background distortion and routed the feed to the speakers Mitchell had procured for the technical rig.

It was only a short clip of audio, but it was all he needed. There was no doubt now that it was Delman's voice, there was no mistaking it. He'd grown up with that voice booming out of the screens, and it was definitely Delman. He was talking to somebody whose voice he didn't recognize. It was a man and whoever he was he sounded much younger than Delman.

It was what they were saying that caught Wiz's attention most. They were clearly concerned with something called the 'Centurial' – Wiz had never heard the word before.

Whatever it was, it was causing President Delman great anxiety. Not only was this event just hours away, but he was also making plans for his own urgent evacuation from The City.

Sabotage

The alarm went off in Max's desk area. Normally it would have raised an amber alert. This time it was a red alert. Immediate action required.

He'd been keeping an eye on the screens feed, cursing when Lucy left her chamber area. The scenario was certainly compelling, and the way she'd escaped Schälen must have made Damien Hunter ecstatic.

For a moment he'd thought his plan would be foiled, until he saw what Schälen was planning to do. He was actually sawing off his own hand. That would mean the camera he'd chosen for the sabotage was ideally placed.

Max couldn't believe his luck when the camera went dark. Talya's friends had managed the hack – it was perfect.

And now the alarm was going off and agitated Fortrillium staff were snarling at him to get it fixed – fast.

This was his chance to get Talya off his back. He'd locate the WristCom, tell her where it was, and let her get a message to her daughter. It wasn't his problem how she did it. His work was over at that stage. He could go back to his quiet life, head down, with nobody noticing him. It was how he liked it. Whenever you got involved with anything complicated you ended up in trouble. He rubbed his hand and gently clenched it. The pain was almost too much to bear. It would be some time before he got full use back, if at all.

Max wondered what Schälen must be going through. Talya had mauled his hand, but she hadn't cut it off. Schälen was hacking through his hand with an instrument that was unsuitable for the job. It was meant for cutting and penetrating flesh, not sawing through bone. Much as he loathed Schälen, he had to admire the man's grit and strength. Max was not at all sure he would have been able to do the same thing.

More orders came over the Comms system, and Max had to act fast. He requested permission to send three maintenance bots into The Grid: it was imperative the broken camera be fixed as soon as possible.

The Fortrillium staff were in such a state about the loss of the live feed on Schälen that they agreed immediately. Max deployed the bots. They'd have to liaise with the Gridders to ensure the route was clear.

Max dispatched the mechanical contraptions up the long, secure tunnel leading to The Grid. No human would ever make it up there – it was a place where only specially enabled machines could navigate.

He sent coordinates and route requirements electronically to Fortrillium, who passed that data to the Gridders to secure a private route through the labyrinth. It was imperative that none of the Justice Seekers came into contact with the bots – that would really land Max in big trouble. He also needed to disable cameras on the route, since it would be unacceptable to have the mechanical devices seen on the screens.

Max waited as the bots made their way into The Grid. He had a rough idea where the WristCom was located. He'd chosen Lucy's original location in the cell area because it was centrally positioned – he knew the device had to be in that general area.

The risk for Max was in activating a visual feed on one of the bots. That was what might have exposed what he was up to. He needed the visual feed to effect the repairs, but the third bot – the one that would not be used to fix the broken camera feed – that was just scanning the ground.

It was relatively easy for Max to judge the positioning of the bots. The Grid appeared as a rectangular graphic on his screen and the bots were indicated by pulsating green dots and the broken camera by a red arrow. It was more confusing for him to see the shape and form of the labyrinth. It was too easy to get disoriented like that.

Max considered how difficult it would be for Talya's daughter to navigate her way around those tunnels. In real life she was just making her way around a giant hangar, but to Lucy and the Justice Seekers it was every bit a real and threatening environment.

The bots neared the centre, and Max dared to activate a light on the unit. It illuminated the dark passageway; he kept his eyes sharp for the WristCom. The other two bots set about making the repairs. The Gridders had contained Schälen within a smaller chamber while the work went ahead. They'd just dropped another wall in the area where he'd previously struggled to reach the knife, and this allowed the bots to do their work unobserved.

The camera repair was easily made. Talya's friends had been good – they'd disabled it temporarily to make it look like a fault, rather than sabotage. That was clever. There would be a complete security lockdown if there was any suspicion that The Grid had been breached.

Max cursed as the bot made its way around the area. It had to be there somewhere, they were in the same part of The Grid that the WristCom had originally been lost.

The camera reactivated, and Max received the directive to withdraw the bots from the immediate area while remote tests were done to make sure the feed had been repaired properly.

He became more anxious as the seconds passed. He was going to miss his chance, and if he couldn't find the WristCom he would have Talya Slater pushing him even harder to come up with a solution. She might even consider handing him over to Fortrillium as a traitor.

The camera was confirmed as fixed, and Max was told to withdraw the bots. He cursed to himself as he keyed in the instructions and the bots made their way back towards the tunnel. He was sweating with the tension. He'd messed up – he couldn't find the WristCom.

As the bots made their way back to Max, he turned to the screen feed on his console. The Gridders removed the wall they'd positioned behind Schälen to stop him detecting the presence of the mechanical intruders. The camera feed returned to him immediately; he was, after all, the most compelling drama in The Grid at that moment. Max's face screwed up as he saw that Schälen had managed to free his crushed hand in the intervening

period. The camera view switched to night vision mode –
the small amount of light Schälen had to work with had
diminished as the flame burned down on the nearest
torch.

As the screen feed went from a dull, shadowed image to
a sharper view, infused with a green hue, Max saw what
he'd been looking for: i

t was the WristCom. He'd been right about its location.
It had to be around that area somewhere. There was just
one problem. Schälen had found it while thrashing around
in the semi-darkness. It was now attached to his wrist, the
one which wasn't bound by bloodied rags.

Schälen had the WristCom, and Talya was going to get
exactly what she wanted. The WristCom was heading
directly to her daughter. There was one thing for sure: now
Schälen was free, the first person he'd be visiting was Lucy
Slater.

Unleashed

It was 20:00 hours, though none of the Justice Seekers knew
that. Stuck in the dark dungeon, they'd lost all concept of
time and place.

Everybody in the main group was alert. They'd chosen
weapons, agreed to a defensive formation, and rehearsed
several scenarios. They didn't know what would happen
next, but they'd heard the roars echoing through the
tunnels. It sounded as if they would be attacked by some
sort of creature in the next Mode. They couldn't guess at
the size or the type of creature, but it would be geared to
drama and excitement for those watching on the screens.

It would always begin with an address from Damien
Hunter. They knew they were safe until then.

'Eat and drink while you can,' Clay had urged. 'We don't know how long we'll have to do without afterwards.'

'Chris, remember, stay in the middle – don't break away. The minute Hunter appears, form a circle, raise your weapons.'

They were well drilled. None of this group were fighters, but they were preparing to battle for their lives.

Joe had agreed with Clay that he'd stay with the group until they knew the nature of the threat, and then he'd break off to try to find Lucy. Ross would accompany him, but only when they knew what they were dealing with.

Joe was practising with his spear when Hunter appeared. It happened so fast – it always did when the Modes began.

There was a bright light. It caught them by surprise, particularly as their eyes had adjusted to the darkness.

Chris threw his hammer at the image of Hunter. It was just a hologram, and the hammer flew straight through the projection, landing somewhere in the darkness.

'Careful, Chris, try to stay calm!' Miron urged, but he was experiencing his own panic attack, and he understood how Chris felt. Damien Hunter tended to have that effect on people.

Hunter's voice boomed all around them.

'An eye for an eye, a tooth for a tooth, a life for a life. So it is in our city that any person who breaks the law shall find justice in The Grid. It has been our way since the plague years. It has kept our city safe and fair for almost one hundred years.'

They'd heard these words dozens of times as The Justice Trials had played out on the screens. Only now they were the ones fighting for their lives.

'Ten Justice Seekers remain in The Grid today. If any

find justice there, they will walk away with their freedom. This is how our society preserves truth and honesty.'

As the words 'truth and honesty' echoed along the tunnels, the Law Lords came into view. Joe immediately noticed that Talya was there. They'd made her a Law Lord – how had that happened, especially with everything going on with Lucy and him? She was choked up and struggling to maintain her composure, but she was staring straight out at them. It was almost as if she was there with them.

Leianna Richwald stepped forward.

'You ten stand charged with crimes against The City. If you find justice in The Grid, you shall walk free.'

Once more, Hunter's voice boomed out, and Richwald stepped back into the line of Law Lords.

'Justice Seekers, find your justice!'

Joe was uncertain of the ordering of the next events, it all happened so fast.

As the holographic images of Hunter and the Law Lords began to fade, they all heard Talya calling out: '

Keep fighting, Lucy. Stay alive!'

Her words were cut off. As they faded away, a deafening noise immediately demanded their attention. Around them doors opened up, three in total, each leading to a long passageway.

Behind one of the doorways was Lucy, standing alert underneath a burning torch, on which was tied Ross's rag.

She saw the group immediately.

'Joe! Run!' she shouted as she turned and fled in their direction.

'Lucy, get into the circle!'

'I've seen them – I was face-to-face with one – they're going to kill us, Joe!'

Joe had never seen Lucy so distressed before. She was almost in a state of blind panic.

The group formed a circle, as they'd planned, with Chris in the middle.

'Lucy, Joe, stand in the middle, take a moment.'

Clay realized they'd need to focus before the battle began. They'd only have seconds to get their minds in the right place.

'Take this hammer, Lucy, and use it if you have to!'

Marjani thrust the weapon into Lucy's hand. 'There's a scythe too if you want it.'

'What happened, Lucy? Where have you been?'

'It's Schälen – the man is a maniac, he was going to kill me.'

'Where is he now?'

'I don't know, I lost him. He may be dead.'

'What did you see out there? What's coming?'

'They put one right next to me, Joe. I could smell its breath and hear its heartbeat. It was just waiting as if it was asleep or something, but it'll be coming for us now. It's huge, it's nearly the height of the tunnels!'

Lucy didn't need to offer any more description. There was a low, predatory growl and the stench of rancid breath. At first, all they could see was a dark shadow. Slowly, the creature got closer, eventually moving into the light.

It was a thing of nightmares. When Lucy encountered it earlier it had been dormant, a new terror waiting to be activated by the Gridders when the next Mode began.

Its long tusks looked even more threatening in the dim light. They thrust outwards, ready to impale whoever stood in their path. The creature's blue eyes shone in the gloom and its sharp, ferocious teeth snapped wildly as it prepared to kill its prey.

'Hold the circle!' shouted Clay. 'If you break it, we'll be picked off one at a time.'

Chris began to sob, and Lucy moved to comfort him. As she did so, Joe saw her arm.

'What did he do to you?' was all he could ask.

The growling creature came closer and closer, eyeing up its opponents and waiting to strike. It looked at Joe and Lucy – it seemed intent on seeking them out.

There was silence in the circle, and all eyes were trained on the beast in front of them. Hearts were pounding furiously, waiting for the moment when the battle would commence. As the creature started to run towards them, two more appeared at the ends of the tunnels leading from each of the doorways.

Then, without warning, a fourth entrance opened up at their rear. There was another creature. There were four in all. Each one the same: huge, dark and terrifying.

Weapons were held out, ready to repel any attack, but the first beast was upon them. As Joe turned to look at the creature that had just appeared at their rear, the first beast charged at Rick, impaling him instantly on one of his tusks. For a few short seconds he struggled, before his body went limp. He was dead.

The creature behind them ran into the group, and in the remaining two passageways the final pair of beasts smelled Rick's blood and began their charge towards the Justice Seekers.

Joe had time for just one thought before he was thrust into the heart of the bloody battle: surely there was no way any of them would make it out alive?

CHAPTER NINE

Conflict

Talya had been unsure about whether to call out to Lucy in the brief moment that she'd been able to speak to her. She wanted Lucy to see her and to make sure she'd caught a glimpse of the pendant, so she would know they were fighting for her.

The stakes were so high, and her efforts seemed to be frustrated at every turn. It was beginning to feel as if Damien Hunter had every exit covered.

Leianna Richwald had actually tutted when she'd called out to Lucy, and it had certainly got the attention of the other Law Lords.

Damien Hunter walked over, smiling. He was clearly feeling more confident now. Talya wondered if she should have confided in him.

'That's not a very clever thing to do, Law Lord Slater. I know you have the President's favour, but the laws surrounding the procedures in Justice Trials are clear and fair. No interventions other than the legally required wording are permitted, and you have violated those restrictions.'

'What did you expect?' she snapped back at him. 'That's my daughter you're about to send in to be murdered.'

'You of all people know the laws of The City, Law Lord Slater. I will have to refer you under legal document 12d, section 4i to the scrutiny of your peers. Law Lord Richwald will lead the proceedings. You will be required to attend for review at 09:00 hours tomorrow morning.'

Talya was annoyed with herself for making the outburst. If she had kept her mouth shut, she might have been more use to Lucy.

'You know of course that you are now placed under a restrictive order for the next twenty-four hours while the review is taking place.'

Talya knew exactly what that meant. No impromptu tours of any Fortrillium facilities, no further Law Lord duties, and no official access to Max Penner for the next day. That could be the difference to Lucy – she might be dead in the next twenty-four hours. Talya should have known better; she'd let her daughter down with her angry outburst.

'I'll get your access restricted straight away. I'm sure you understand?'

Damien Hunter enjoyed saying those words. It was all Talya could do not to punch him, but she contained herself. That would cause even more trouble.

'I understand,' she said. 'I'm sorry, I don't know what came over me there. I was just so overwhelmed by the situation.'

Damien nodded, and for a fleeting second she even believed he was sympathetic.

'I'll need to downgrade your access level until the review is complete. You won't be able to enter the Fortrillium building again until tomorrow.'

'Understood. I'll be here tomorrow morning.'

The other Law Lords started to move away, sensing the main spectacle was over. Law Lord Sivil seemed distracted by what had just happened. Leianna Richwald left the area with a smirk on her face – that was another person Talya was ready to punch. She had Talya's fate in her hands, so there was little point in antagonizing her. Talya would play along with them, she'd be fully compliant, she needed her privileges back.

As the room cleared, she moved a little closer to Hunter.

'You know, we can still work this thing out,' she said quietly.

'Don't ever think I won't negotiate, Damien, whenever you're ready to sit down and talk. It doesn't have to be this way.'

Damien didn't meet her eyes, but she sensed a small nod.

'09:00 hours tomorrow, Law Lord Slater,' he replied. 'I look forward to seeing you again then.'

He didn't bite. Talya wondered what was wrong with the man. Why was he so difficult to reach?

Hunter left the room, and Talya was on her own. Two Centuria arrived – they were there to escort her from the building. She was accompanied to a point well beyond the security gates of the Fortrillium building. Damien Hunter couldn't have sent a clearer message if he'd tried. There were no deals to be made. He still considered Talya the enemy.

It was dark, and Talya needed to head back home to catch up with the latest developments on the screens. The new Mode had begun – who knew what Lucy and Joe were facing in there? She wondered about Max Penner, Wiz and Mitchell. Had they made any progress while she'd been attending to her Law Lord duties?

Absorbed in her thoughts, she was barely aware of the dark figures coming up behind her in the darkness. It was seldom necessary to worry about personal security on Silk Road, and Talya never feared for her safety while walking alone at night.

They were upon her in a moment. Her own thoughts were elsewhere, and they got to her in the same instant she'd realized that there was even a threat.

Talya was injected with a drug which immediately rendered her unconscious and thrown into a black, window-less van that had been parked a little further along the road.

As her daughter fought for survival in the darkness of the labyrinth, at that very moment it was Talya's life which seemed to be the one under more immediate threat.

Treachery

Mitchell was aware that Wiz was trying to contact him, but he didn't want to talk. As soon as he'd left The Climbs and made his way to the security gate, he'd been met by Teanna Schaelles who was waiting for him in a black car. She knew where he was and what he'd been doing – they were watching him from afar.

She'd been keen to talk to him alone before they reached the President.

'We were very interested to hear you are friends with Talya Slater and Hannah James,' she began, not bothering with pleasantries.

'We've been monitoring Law Lord Slater. She seems to be very good friends with Mr Hunter.'

Mitchell fell right into the trap.

'Not a chance! She loathes the man. She blames him for the death of her husband. It's because of Hunter that we got involved in all of this.'

'You've done some remarkable work to infiltrate Fortrillium, Mitchell. Your friends must be extremely grateful for your expertise. I can see you'd be highly suited to a senior role within the President's office – he's always looking for talented people like you.'

Mitchell could barely contain his pride. Imagine being able to boast about being headhunted by the President of all people! That was above Fortrillium, it was incredibly prestigious.

'How is Hannah doing?' Teanna asked, gliding seamlessly between flattery and information gathering. Mitchell was no match for her.

'Talya made contact with her at Fortrillium – at least she knows Joe and Lucy are in there now.'

'You've done well, Mitchell. Thank you for your updates.

As you know, this information is crucial to President Delman and he's extremely grateful for everything you're doing. You'll be well rewarded, of course, and your friends are protected. It's important that we track down the source of these leaks in Fortrillium.

It's likely they lead directly to Damien Hunter. You could be doing the citizens of The City a great service, Mitchell.'

Mitchell nodded. It felt good to be working at this level, alongside the President. He only wished he could share the information with his friends and family.

As he considered the excitement of his current situation, Teanna's tone changed and she leaned towards him in the vehicle.

'Mitchell, I don't want you to mention Hannah James when you speak to the President. Is that understood?'

Mitchell was surprised by these words, he wasn't expecting a request like that. Teanna's tone made it clear this was a statement rather than a question. He didn't know what to do or say. He just nodded.

They travelled in silence until they reached the President's offices, then Teanna excused herself. Mitchell was taken aback, but guessed the President would want to talk to him alone.

The President was genial as ever and very complimentary about Mitchell's technical abilities. Mitchell felt that Joe, Lucy and Wiz took him for granted much of the time, and it was good to be acknowledged for his contribution. Even better that it was by the President.

'I'm interested to hear a little more about Talya Slater and your friend Hannah,' he began. 'We've been unable to find out much about them. Hunter keeps himself very much to himself.'

Mitchell went for the easy option first, explaining the events of the day and the progress made.

'That's really quite excellent, Mitchell. I can see how your friend – Wiz, isn't it? – I can see how he relies on you so much to help him out.'

Mitchell felt vindicated. At last somebody who saw his true contribution and value.

'Are you any closer to retrieving the data from those files?'

'Not yet. Wiz is working on it tonight, but I don't think he'll get very far without me there.'

Mitchell was beginning to believe the praise that was being heaped upon him.

'We didn't make a massive amount of progress today, other than to get our infrastructure set up. I think things will start to move tomorrow.'

The President nodded, and then his eyes narrowed.

'You haven't told me anything about Hannah James yet. How is she connected with all of this?'

Mitchell felt a bead of sweat trickle down from just above his temple. He hoped the President hadn't seen it. He gulped, concealing it as well as he could.

'Not much to report, sir. She's working as a Gridder, as far as I know, but she's stuck in there until the trial ends. We can't talk to her, and she can't talk to us.'

President Delman said nothing. He waited in silence until Mitchell became too uncomfortable.

'Nobody has managed to contact her, I'm afraid.'

Were they testing him? Is that why Teanna had asked him to keep his mouth shut about Hannah? Should he reveal to the President that Hannah and Talya had spoken?

Another trickle of sweat ran down his cheek.

'It's very warm in here,' he said by way of cover. Mitchell doubted that Delman had been fooled.

'You are telling me everything, I hope?' Delman asked. 'I'd hate you to curtail your prospects in this office by withholding information. You know how important it is for me to monitor Damien Hunter's activities?'

Mitchell considered his options. To tell or not to tell? Teanna had been very clear earlier. It didn't sound as if she wanted him to deceive the President, it had just seemed she didn't want him troubled by this information.

He made his mind up as Teanna walked through the wooden door and entered the office.

'Mx Schaelles, thank you for joining us,' said Delman. 'Mitchell was just telling me how there's no progress to report on Hannah James. That's a shame, isn't it?'

Teanna didn't even look at Mitchell. She kept her face straight and answered as if nothing had happened.

'That's unfortunate, sir. Hopefully the situation will change soon.'

'I think we're done here, Mitchell. We don't have a lot of time left, and I'll be relying on you to make some progress by the time we talk again tomorrow.'

He checked himself. He was beginning to threaten. It was his default style, and this wasn't what was required to best motivate this particular person.

'I know we can rely on you to progress this little project of yours. I'm sure your friend Wiz will be grateful when you're able to rejoin him once again.'

Mitchell and Teanna were dismissed with a nod, and Teanna accompanied Mitchell to the waiting vehicle outside.

'I didn't say anything—'

'Shh!' Teanna hissed back. 'Keep your voice down!'

Mitchell stopped talking immediately and continued to walk with Teanna.

They climbed into the car and drove through the security gates as they had done on the previous day. But instead of accelerating away, the vehicle took a turn, moving into the park and woodland area that lay beyond the gates of the President's offices. It pulled to the side of the road where a truck was waiting, its lights dimmed.

Mitchell's instincts immediately told him he was in danger. His hand moved to the door handle, but it was locked, there was no escape. He actually looked at Teanna, as if she was going to supply him with an explanation.

She remained silent, then indicated to the driver that he should let her out of the car. It was too dark for Mitchell to see what was going on, but he knew it wasn't good.

What had he done? Had he exposed his friends and put them at risk? Of course he had, but he'd thought he was helping the President.

They'd got him, but was this what the President wanted or did Teanna Schaelles have an agenda of her own? Mitchell didn't have any of the answers, but he knew he had to get a message to Wiz and Talya fast.

He typed a warning swiftly into his WristCom, keeping his hand low so the driver wouldn't figure out what he was up to. It was too late anyway – his door was being opened.

His heart almost stopped beating when he saw who was with Teanna outside the vehicle. There were four Centuria, a full Quad Team, armed and looking more threatening than they'd ever looked to Mitchell before. They patted him down and tore off his WristCom. One reached into the car and retrieved his bag of tech.

Mitchell was thrown into the back of the truck. There was no attempt to make it easy for him. He was not a guest there – it looked as if he was about to become a prisoner. He retreated as far back as he could. He wanted to keep as great a distance as possible between him and the guards.

Was this what the President wanted? He thought not. Centuria were Fortrillium employees, and the President had his own guards. It was never good news if the Centuria were around, but what did Teanna Schaelles have to do with the Centuria?

Mitchell got his explanation moments later. Another vehicle drew up alongside the truck. Out of it stepped Damien Hunter. He embraced Teanna then turned to

Mitchell, who was now cowering in the furthest corner of the vehicle.

'Welcome, Mitchell. How lovely to meet you!'

Teanna smiled at that. It looked like this was all pre-planned.

'I'm going to have a little chat with you, Mitchell. Let's call it a getting-to-know-you session. I'm going to ask some questions and you're going to answer truthfully. Now, we already know you're a nasty little rat who'd ditch his friends at the slightest hint of flattery.'

Mitchell felt shamed and fooled. How stupid he'd been, they'd been playing him all along.

'We can do this the easy way or we can do it the hard way.

In fact, I'm busy. We'll just do it the hard way – I want to encourage you to tell the truth. Teanna tells me you've already lied to the President this evening, and I want you to understand that is something I refuse to accept.'

One of the Centuria handed Damien a black case, and he took it and placed it on the floor of the truck. Damien hoisted himself up into the truck, and then stood right on the edge looking intently at Mitchell.

He picked up the case, opening it slowly and deliber-ately. He meant to intimidate Mitchell and it was working. He walked slowly up to him and then signalled to the Centuria. Two of them helped Teanna up into the back of the truck, then climbed up there themselves.

One of the Centuria standing guard outside the vehicle reached up and closed the doors. They were heavy and thick – nobody would hear what was going on. The rear of the truck was fully lit. Mitchell was dazzled as he looked directly at the four people in front of him.

Damien opened the case, then turned it round so

Mitchell could see what was inside it. He didn't bother to do a full inventory, he got the gist of what was about to happen. The steel implements caught the light as Hunter brought the case directly up to Mitchell's face.

'So, let's get started, shall we, Mitchell? I'm going to ask you some questions about Hannah James and Talya Slater. Every time I ask a question, I'm going to encourage a full and frank answer with one of the implements in this case.

'The question is not if I will use them, only how many I will use.

'So let's get started, shall we?'

Contact

Wiz would have liked to have had some company in the apartment, but once again he was on his own. Just like the previous night, he'd been abandoned by Mitchell, and Jena and Dillon were nowhere to be seen.

He wasn't sure what to do with the new information. There was something very serious going on with Delman, but he didn't have enough information to work with.

He attempted to contact Talya. Her WristCom was blocked – she was probably busy with Law Lord duties. He tried Mitchell's WristCom. Again, no response, the device was blocked for incoming messages.

Silk Roaders seemed to be able to just step away from a crisis. He'd had no sleep, and he was struggling not to become resentful of the others.

'It's all about Lucy and Joe,' he repeated to himself, flicking to the screen feed to see how his friends were faring. The camera feed was back again – he hoped Talya's contact had done whatever he needed to do. The serial killer was free again. He wasn't anywhere near Joe and Lucy, but he was on the move.

Wiz wasn't sure what to do next. He'd have to discuss his discovery about the Centurial with Talya – they needed to find out what that was. Why was Delman making plans to leave The City? Nobody left The City, there was nothing out there. He'd heard Delman tell them himself on the screens. They were lucky to have sanctuary within its walls; there was nothing but death and ruin in the world outside.

Wiz decided the best course of action was to work on Matt's files. He'd monitor the screen feed, leave Delman's communication line open in case he used it again, then try to find out whatever Matt had been hiding.

It didn't take him long to get back into the files, but it was worrying him that somebody in Fortrillium had tried to lock them again. Was Fortrillium on to them? They'd seized Lucy and Joe's tech when they were taken by the Centuria, and they must have had a pretty good idea what they were looking at. Fortrillium didn't know that Wiz had access. He'd managed to avoid detection so far, and they were oblivious that he'd been down in the sewers to secure his feeds.

The encryption had been easy to crack. Wiz still had the DNA-based release codes saved, so the files were still accessible. Fortrillium would not be able to access Matt's secret data, it was invisible to them, they didn't even know it existed yet. Wiz moved around the Fortrillium folders – there was so much he didn't understand, and he wished Talya or Mitchell were around to guide him through it.

Wiz was on secure ground when it came to the tech. He typed away, moving through the data, looking for something he could use. Then he saw it. Matt had been clever. He'd known that Fortrillium might access the information if he was captured, so he'd added this extra level of encryption. The reason Wiz couldn't find anything was because there was nothing to find. That's how Matt had left it. But these were mirrored files.

He was looking at a digital reflection. The real files were in Matt's secure area, but invisible. Wiz knew this technique well. It was in common use among the few tech users in The Climbs; it was a dark technology which they would not use on Silk Road. How had Matt known about that? Did it matter? Wiz could access the files. It would just be a matter of time until he worked out the encryption cipher.

There was a commotion outside the apartment. He'd been aware of the booming voices from the outdoor speakers, and he could tell there was a lot of excitement about whatever drama was playing out on the screens. There were several windows missing in Harry's apartment – decay and neglect meant that several glass panes had fallen out over the years, crashing onto the ground below.

Old plastic, rotten wood and rusted corrugated iron sheets often had to suffice instead, but it meant Wiz was aware of what was happening outside much of the time. He was high up in the apartment, so he only got a general sense of what was going on, but the change in atmosphere was enough to make him stop his work and look down.

There were armed teams of Centuria gathering below in the square. They didn't seem to be there for the crowds watching the screens – there was no unrest, no sign of any incidents.

His WristCom sounded an alert. It was Mitchell at last. There was just a short message, and it told Wiz everything he needed to know: 'Get out of there, they're coming for you. I'm sorry.'

Damn Mitchell. What had he done? The Centuria

were out there for him. He was so close to getting into the files, and now Mitchell had messed things up.

How long until they reached Wiz's floor? He worked it out. They'd often race themselves to see how fast they could run up the stairways. The Centuria were armed and had to carry heavy outfits. They'd be slower than Wiz, Lucy and Joe.

He reckoned at least ten minutes. He was nearly in. If he could break into the files and send them to Talya, at least she would know what to do with the information.

Wiz typed fast at his console. He was so close, but they were on to him, there was no time left. If only he'd realized what Matt had done sooner, they'd have had more time to work with the information. Matt had had to make it secure, of course he had, and he must have had a lot of faith in Joe to think he'd finally be able to crack the encryption.

Well, Joe was gone, and it was up to him. He'd seen them enter the building moments before, as he looked down from Harry's apartment. How long would it take them to reach him? They wouldn't move as fast as Wiz could – they had equipment to carry, those black suits to wear. He had ten minutes surely, maybe even as much as fifteen, if he got lucky. He'd never considered having no elevators a blessing, but today he was grateful that everybody had to use the stairs. It might just save some lives. If he could just see what Matt had left them and send it over to Talya, it wouldn't matter so much if they got him now. Talya would be able to take it from there if it came to that.

He kept entering the codes, cursing that Mitchell had betrayed his whereabouts. What had he been offered in return? What had made it worth forsaking his companions and sending them to almost certain death? Wiz hoped

Mitchell could live with himself after this. He thought they'd been friends. He'd been sure they were friends.

Every time he entered a new password, an obstructing beep would sound on his console, denying him access. He pictured the staircase, trying to assess how far the Centuria would have made it by now. Level 10 maybe, Level 15 at the most, and there was debris at Level 17 – that slowed everybody down.

Then there was a different electronic sound. He almost missed it, he was so used to being blocked. His console began to run a program; it was like nothing he'd ever seen before, and he wasn't sure what was happening. It took about half a minute. The device drew what little solar power it had managed to store in Harry's apartment and, like a ghost from another world, a holographic image of Matt appeared in front on him. He looked tired and bloody.

Wiz had never known Matt personally; his death was before he'd even met Joe, but he realized who it was anyway, there was only one person it could be. He wished Joe could see this – he knew how much he'd have liked to see his own father again.

The image was unstable, and Matt had taken a few moments before he'd started to speak. Wiz heard the smashing of debris from the stairwell out on the landing – they'd reached Level 17. He hoped he'd have enough time to catch the message.

'Joe, if you're watching this you've turned into the man I knew you'd become. I'm so sorry about what happened, but when I tell you what was going on you'll understand why I did what I had to do. Joe, I wish I could be with you. It was the hardest thing I've ever had to do in my life to leave you, Dillon and Jena. But if you're watching this now, it could soon be over. You must never let Fortrillium know about this, Joe, whatever they try to do to you. If they know what I'm about to tell you, it will all be over. Joe, I know this will be difficult for you but ...'

The holographic image of Matt hesitated – he seemed to be a man who had a lot on his mind. He stared directly into Wiz's eyes, and it was almost as if he was there. The sound of heavy boots could be heard thundering up the stairwell – there wasn't much time now.

'Joe, this will be difficult to believe, but you have to trust me. I know what you saw on the screens. I know what everybody saw. But the truth is, Joe, it was all a deception. I'm still alive, Joe, and you need to come to me now ...'

Wiz was stunned by Matt's message. What else would he discover in those files if this is what he'd seen first? He was out of time – he could hear the approaching footsteps.

He could send the access codes to Talya, but would she know what to do with them? Dillon might help, but his tech skills were nowhere near as good as they needed to be. What about Hannah? Could Talya use her skills to access the data?

Wiz cursed Mitchell once again – what had he done to get them discovered? He needed to send this data to Mitchell, but was it safe?

Wiz was out of time, and he had to make his decision. He compressed the files, encrypted them, and sent them over a secure channel using the WristCom, just as Mitchell had shown him earlier. He wished he had time to add a message – that would have to suffice.

The Centuria were three, maybe two floors away, just enough time to record a short video message to Talya: 'Not safe here now. Mitchell to blame – don't know what he's done. Matt is alive – you need to access files. Try Dillon or

Hannah. Be careful with Mitchell. Sorry, I hope Joe and Lucy get out.'

The thudding of boots stopped suddenly on the staircase and a single weapon was fired. It sounded random. The shots were hitting metalwork and mortar. It didn't sound like Centuria.

Whatever it was, it had gained Wiz some precious time. He seized his main console and threw anything else that might be useful to the Centuria out of the window. He ran out of the apartment onto the stairwell, daring to peer down to see what was holding up the Centuria.

He saw a hand dart out. It was a woman's hand. He recognized the weapon too.

'Jena?' he called down. 'Is that you?'

'Run for it, Wiz!' she called back. 'Take Dillon.'

'I'm not leaving you on your own, Jena ...'

'Shut up, Wiz. Take Dillon and go. Nothing matters if they get to you. Just run for it and keep fighting.'

Dillon ran up the staircase towards Wiz. He'd never heard Jena speak like that before – he never thought she had it in her. Dillon looked terrified, his face grey with fear.

Jena was right. If they all got captured by the Centuria, there was nothing any of them could do to help themselves or Joe and Lucy. Jena would be taken, but at least she would go out fighting. Dillon could still get out of this and so could Wiz if they were fast enough to think of a way out. Dillon had brought the power packs too – that was good.

He had to run. It was the only way.

'Move now!' Jena shouted. 'I can't hold them off much longer!'

Wiz grabbed Dillon's arm.

'Come with me, we're getting out of here. Grab those old sacks in the corner, we're going to need them.'

Dillon didn't argue. He picked up the discarded sacks and followed Wiz.

'We're heading up a few floors first. Then we need to get down again.'

The two fugitives ran as fast as they could up the stairs, Dillon lagging slightly behind.

'Come on, Dillon!' Wiz shouted, as Jena fired another shot several floors below. Wiz counted eleven floors, then moved across to the elevator area.

'Help me with these,' he shouted at Dillon as he began to force the elevator doors apart. There was another shot below, and Wiz could hear more boots in the stairwell, but they weren't making progress yet. It was just more Centuria ready to charge the staircase once Jena had been immobilized.

'We need something to force them open,' said Dillon, moving back to the stairs.

'Don't go down, you'll run into them.'

'There's an old iron bar from the staircase there. I saw it on the way up.'

'Okay, get it, but be quick!

Wiz continued to try to push open the doors and managed to force a small gap. Dillon swiftly returned with the bar. Wiz took it off him and forced it into the narrow gap.

'Help me,' he said, moving his hands along the bar so Dillon could join him. They pushed hard and the doors opened.

'Tear the sacks and wrap the cloth around your hands – we're sliding down the wire.'

Dillon looked at him, doubtful for a moment, but then spurred on by the sound of another shot from Jena.

'That's her out of shots. They'll figure it out in a few minutes. We've got to go now. You going first or second?'

'I'll come behind you,' said Dillon, torn between making his escape and going back to Jena.

'You're going first,' Wiz replied, pushing him towards the open doors. 'You're not going back down there – this is the only way. You need to jump for the cable and slide down slowly or your hands will burn. Take your time. The elevator looks like it's stuck at level 20 or thereabouts – wait for me there.'

Dillon stood on the edge, looking down at the drop more than twenty levels below to the jammed elevator. He jumped but messed up the leap. He caught the cable with one hand but missed with the other. He'd got enough grip to hang on, but no traction. He was beginning to slide down the wire.

'Grab it with your other hand!' Wiz called down. 'Slow yourself down.' Dillon forced out his free hand at waist level and managed to grip the cable, slowing down his descent. The sacking around one hand was shredded and burnt, but he managed to steady himself and begin a slower descent.

'You okay?' shouted Wiz.

'Yes, I'm good. Take care when you leap – it's further out than it looks.'

It was Wiz's turn. He placed the power packs in his bag. He'd need those later. He had to try to close the doors to put the Centuria off their scent when they came up the stairwell. They'd shoot down the shaft or apprehend them at the bottom of the apartment block if they realized how they'd made their escape. Wiz wanted them to search all of the levels above Harry's first, including the roof, before they thought about the elevator shaft. It would buy them some time.

With his bag of tech slung across his shoulders and now feeling much heavier, Wiz forced the left-hand door shut once again. Moving to the right-hand side, he stood on the edge of the shaft, then dropped towards the cable, keeping his feet on the ground. For once, he thanked his good fortune for being so tall. He was able to hang on to the cable with his feet still right at the edge of the stairwell floor. Straddled across the dark elevator shaft, he slowly moved his right foot to the top of the elevator. Tensing his body, he moved his left foot to the door, then pushed as hard as he could to close the gap. It took some effort, but the door closed, and as it did it removed all light from the elevator shaft.

'Is everything okay?' shouted Dillon. He was making good progress.

'Yes, keep going. I'm coming up behind you,' said Wiz, kicking his feet away from the closed door and taking his full weight on the cable with his arms. Slowly, he began the descent behind Dillon, in silence and complete blackness.

Several floors below, the first Centuria ventured up the stairwell towards Jena. When there was no weapon fire, they rushed up the stairs. Jena had taken sanctuary in Harry's apartment, knowing it was only a matter of time.

The first Centuria in the room shot at her immediately, paralysing Jena instantly with a blast from his weapon. Three electric bolts lodged in her chest, blasting her with a massive charge as she dropped to the ground.

Centuria swarmed into the room, seizing all of the remaining equipment and removing Jena's limp body on a stretcher.

They moved in formation up the staircases, bursting into occupied apartments and searching every available space for the two fugitives.

Whatever Mitchell had done, he'd blown apart Lucy and Joe's best hope of escape. And now Jena was a captive – for all Wiz knew she was dead. As he made his way down the long, cold elevator shaft, he cursed the so-called friend who'd betrayed them. Mitchell had probably killed all of them with his treachery.

CHAPTER TEN

Battle

One half of Rick's torn body was tossed back towards the terrified group, landing in the centre of the circle they'd formed. These beasts didn't seem to want to eat, they just wanted to kill.

'Keep the circle tight!' came Clay's voice. 'If we break it, they'll pick us off one by one.'

Chris was becoming very agitated. His overalls were spattered with Rick's blood.

'I need to fight,' Lucy shouted to Joe. 'We'll have to leave Chris in the middle – we're all dead if we don't kill these things.'

Two of the beasts made a second charge, and this time they were ready. Grace pushed out her spear and Miron swung his hammer at the beast's head. It roared with pain and retreated. At least they could be hurt.

On the other side, the second beast had been more successful. Ross, Marjani and Clay managed to spear it twice between them, and again it retreated. The other two beasts rushed straight in, barely giving any time to breathe. They seemed incensed by the green of Joe and Lucy's overalls, as if driven by an obsession to reach them. Joe and Lucy had joined the circle now, and they worked together to force their spears into the creature's head. It screeched with pain, its tusks flailing madly, one narrowly missing Joe, who stepped back just in time. Ross followed up swiftly by running at the creature and pounding its head with a hammer.

'Don't break the circle!' shouted Clay, but it was too late. The beast that had killed Rick charged once again, this time directly towards the side of the circle Ross had broken. Clay saw that their defensive strategy had been disrupted and rushed to help Ross finish off the beast. He thrust his spear directly through the creature's eye. It screamed out then died.

Chris had run off in terror along one of the tunnels of the labyrinth. Lucy saw him go but was too preoccupied with the creature that had killed Rick. It had tasted blood. It seemed more ferocious than the others. The presence of Joe and Lucy seemed to make the creatures frantic – it was as if their presence agitated them even more. Joe and Marjani stabbed and pounded the beast, but it seemed to be exhilarated by the fight and grew stronger and wilder. With a sudden swipe of its deadly tusks, it lifted Marjani high into the air and pounded her body into the roof of the labyrinth, dashing her head against the damp stonework.

She had begun to let out a scream but was dead before it was finished.

'Clay, any ideas?' shouted Joe, not even knowing where he was in the confusion.

'This isn't working,' Clay replied, thrusting a scythe at

one of the creatures. 'We should try fighting in the tunnels – we'll need to splinter into groups and pick them off.'

Joe counted quickly to see who was still left. Chris had run off, probably the best thing for everybody, he was safer like that. Clay, Lucy, Miron, Ross and Grace were still fighting, and one creature was dead. The beast that had killed Marjani had stormed up a long tunnel as if it were some sort of victory ceremony, but at least it meant there were only two of them left to tackle and six Justice Seekers to do the work.

Ross ran at one of the wounded animals, striking again and putting it on the defensive. It tossed its tusks at him, tearing a bloody gash in his leg. He cried out with the pain, but still he fought, pounding the animal as if he'd gone insane. Joe ran up towards him, and when the beast's head was on the floor, Joe plunged his spear into its brain, killing it instantly.

'Are you okay?' he asked Ross. The wound looked bad.

'It hurts like hell, but those teeth would hurt worse!'

Joe smiled. It seemed inappropriate, bearing in mind the death and carnage all around them, but he knew what Ross meant. What option did they have other than to fight for their lives?

'Let's draw them apart!' shouted Clay. 'Joe, you take that tunnel.'

Clay indicated to Miron and Grace to follow him while Joe, Lucy and Ross made their way up another passageway. There were two creatures left, and the Gridders looked like they wanted to mix things up a bit. The tunnels began to change around them: exits were shut off, and new doorways were opened – they were trying to disorient the Justice Seekers.

'Damn Fortrillium!' cursed Lucy. Her arm was red raw

and stiffening – she wondered how long it would continue to be of use to her in a fight.

Along the dark passageways, the roars of the remaining two beasts could be heard. They were further away now, out of sight, but they would be hunting them, they would not stop.

'What's the best strategy?' asked Joe, glancing at Ross and Lucy. Ross looked to be in too much pain to care much, and Lucy was in a bad state too. With no Clay to advise them, he took the lead. '

These things are going to stalk us now. That's what Fortrillium wants. We've lost Rick and Marjani, but they won't let us all die. That's why they've changed the tunnels to stop the bloodbath. We need to ambush, not hunt, they're too strong.'

'Agreed,' replied Ross. 'I can't move too far with this leg – it hurts like hell, but my arms are good.'

'Okay, Ross, I'm going to act as bait and we'll drive the creature towards you. They seem to be incensed by Lucy and me. You stay over there in the dark, with a spear pointing outwards. Lucy and I will drive it towards you.'

Ross moved towards the edge of the tunnel wall, positioning the spear outwards as Joe had suggested.

'Now we just wait.'

'I'm concerned about Chris,' said Lucy. 'They'll kill him straight away if they find him.'

'I know, I know. We'll have to leave it to chance for now. We can't split off anymore – they'll pick us off one by one.'

'And Schälen is still out there too, remember. I'm not sure who to be more afraid of.'

'With any luck, they'll get to him first,' came Ross's voice from the darkness.

A loud scream echoed along the tunnels. It sounded like Grace.

They waited in the darkness, the silence punctuated by screams and roars. It was difficult to tell what was going on, but they stuck to the plan.

It felt as if they'd been waiting for hours, though it was only a matter of minutes. Lucy noticed it first, and she indicated with her eyes to Joe. She had smelled its breath before she saw it. Its tusks still carried the fleshy remains from Rick and Marjani. Then they saw its cold, blue eyes.

'Ross!' Joe whispered. 'Get ready.'

This was the strongest creature and it knew how to hunt. It had quietly moved along the labyrinth's tunnels, stalking its prey, waiting for the moment to strike. But Lucy and Joe had seen it first.

Lucy raised her spear and plunged it into the beast's head as it stepped around the corner into the tunnel. It let out a deafening roar, moving its tusks and knocking her over with the force. She'd avoided the tusks, but the sideways blow winded her. She struggled to recover as the beast moved closer, sensing an easy kill.

Joe ran towards the creature, plunging his spear into its back before it reached Lucy, who was breathless and dazed.

A wall came crashing down between Lucy and the beast. Fortrillium was separating them off, it was denying them the option to fight together. At least Lucy was safe from that creature, but it left Joe and Ross to fight it alone.

Joe tore his spear out of the monster's back, running up along the course of its spine to retrieve the weapon Lucy had left in its head. She must have missed the brain, but the monstrosity was bleeding badly now.

Its wounds seemed to fuel its anger, and Joe dodged

from side to side as it raised its tusks, desperately trying to impale its prey as it had done so effectively before.

'This way. Come over here!' Joe goaded, luring the creature in Ross's direction.

'You ready, Ross? Here we come.'

The beast looked directly at Joe, snarling and snapping its teeth. Then it began its charge, the tusks moving wildly from side to side. Joe could see the spot where Ross was positioned. He ran directly towards it. As he neared Ross, he tossed Lucy's spear at him. Ross caught it and extended it outwards with the other, nestling them in the corner between wall and floor to hold them securely.

The creature ran directly at them, and at the last possible moment, when the tusks were about to plunge deep into Joe's body, he moved out of the way, leaving the beast no time to stop.

It crashed into Ross's spears, both of which cut straight into its neck. Joe leapt on top of the monster and thrust his spear deep into its brain. For a few seconds it was motionless, impaled on Ross's weapons and stunned by Joe's attack.

Then it sank, heavy and lifeless, one tusk either side of Ross who was still sitting against the wall of the labyrinth. It took a moment or two before they both began to breathe again.

'Nice one, Joe!'

'Good job, Ross. I thought it was going to be too strong for us. We've lost Lucy again, though. Did you see what happened? They're splitting us up, and I'm worried about Schälen – she doesn't have a weapon anymore.'

'She can look after herself, but we'd better try and find her. Do you think Clay managed to kill the other creature?'

'Difficult to tell. We'll need to keep listening – they

could be anywhere in here. They haven't changed the Mode yet. The trial must still be ongoing. Let's head out and find Lucy. Are you alright to walk ?'

'Yes, I'm good. I'll use Lucy's spear as a stick. It'll help to keep some weight off it.'

It was a struggle to retrieve the spears from the creature's flesh. It was tough and sinewy – it had been much easier when the blades had slid in.

Ross managed to stand up again, stepping over the creature's tusks, and started making his way with Joe along the tunnels. It made no difference which tunnel they chose. There was no telling which way they were heading in the labyrinth.

Joe tried to work his way back around to where he thought Lucy had been before the wall had crashed down and separated them, but it was no use. There was no sign of her anywhere.

Warily, they made their way along the passageways, with spears at the ready. Occasionally the eerie silence would be interrupted by a scream or a roar, but they were too far away. It was like chasing echoes trying to reunite with the other group.

This continued for some time. Joe felt they were being steered by Fortrillium – doors would open and tunnels close; they were walking in circles.

Suddenly, a loud roar came from behind them. They turned fast, spears at the ready. Something moved in the shadows by their feet.

At first Joe thought it might be rats. He'd seen enough of them in his time living in The Climbs. But whatever had come to rest by their feet was not living. Joe turned to the side to allow the light from the nearest torch to illuminate the object.

He gasped as he saw Grace Makins' severed head which had just rolled along the tunnel. The monster that had killed her had begun its charge at them. It had taken them by surprise, it was almost upon them.

They'd got caught in an ambush and they weren't ready. The creature had tasted blood and now it wanted more.

Combat

There was a spontaneous round of applause the moment Grace's head was torn from her body and was sent rolling towards Joe's feet.

Hannah had engineered that move – she intended to put her friends in as much peril as possible without killing them. It was a difficult thing to do. The beasts were programmed to hunt and kill, and it was impossible to control their every movement, so Joe and Lucy also had to fight for their own survival.

With each execution, Hannah felt a part of herself dying too. There was only so long she would be able to make these kills. She and Linwood worked together, and the other Gridders supported with code inserts and workarounds.

There had been a gasp in the room when Rick died – nobody had expected such an early death. It was a good one too, and there was an expectation among the other Gridders that the engagement levels would be soaring. This was accomplished gameplay.

When Marjani had been pounded to death, that had been done by Linwood, who'd seen his chance to take out another Justice Seeker, avoiding those in the green overalls, the traitors, Joe and Lucy.

But Hannah knew that each death was a human life

lost. This was far from entertainment, it was a public execution. She'd cursed as one of the support Gridders isolated Lucy; it would look good in terms of gameplay, but she wanted her close to Joe at all times.

The severed head was a distraction – the more horrific the deaths of the other Gridders, the more she could make it appear as if her friends were in the thick of the action. If only she could keep Joe and Lucy alive until the next Mode, it would give Talya and Linwood more time to figure things out. The beasts couldn't keep away from Joe and Lucy – they seemed incensed by their presence. That was not Hannah and Linwood's doing.

Hannah thanked her lucky stars that she'd found Linwood, he was proving as good as his word. He was working well with her. They had to make kills, they couldn't avoid it, but between them they'd managed to steer Joe and Lucy clear of danger. Only now another of the Gridders had opened a doorway right next to Joe. She knew it must be Joe, as the pixelated figure on her screen was male with green overalls.

The Gridders were getting carried away with the game, and there was no way she could control them. This was Linwood's Mode to steer. He'd taken on Hannah as his second, but the other Gridders had to be deployed too, and they were the wild card in this.

On the main screen in the office, Hannah scrutinized the set-up of the scene. Joe's companion had a low health rating; he'd lost a lot of blood, and he was badly wounded. Joe's health was fair but his heart rate had gone up dramatically. His energy levels were severely depleted. She could see he was tiring. The creature's adrenalin flow was high, and it would be difficult to beat, given that its opponents were severely weakened.

Could she distort the labyrinth once again, removing Joe from the imminent threat? That would look too obvious – in terms of audience engagement, this was a strong scenario.

She checked on the location of the other Justice Seekers. They were close by distance, but the tunnel networks meant they couldn't reach each other. She considered opening up an exit, allowing the other team to join Joe and help him fight.

There were three other Justice Seekers on her screen. Lucy had to be the female, in green overalls. The serial killer was there too and the man from the Institute who'd run off at the beginning of the first fight. She had limited scope to help out, and the best bet seemed to be to steer the remaining pair towards Joe and his companion – the four of them should be able to kill the remaining creature.

Hannah moved her attention back to her console and began to enter the code to create a new environment. She'd make it look good, not too obvious, but she'd make sure they could find Joe.

She programmed in the data, then entered the activation command. Nothing happened. She ran a quick check to make sure nobody had locked the operation. No locks in place. The gameplay should have been hers.

Without wanting to draw attention to the problem, she sent Linwood a console-to-console text alert. He ran some checks and confirmed all was clear for Hannah's update.

She tried the activation command again. It was blocked. She'd lost control of the environment. Somebody was interfering with The Justice Trial, and whoever they were they were not doing it via a Fortrillium console.

Resistance

Talya's body convulsed violently, and immediately the memories of those final moments came back to her. She'd been attacked from behind, and something injected into her neck. She'd seen Centuria – had they abducted her?

She struggled to focus her mind through the haze left by the drugs but was unable to break through her disorientation. She was freezing – she was wrapped in a blanket, but couldn't shake off the cold.

'Welcome back, Talya,' came a voice. It seemed friendly at least.

She blinked, trying to take in what was going on around her. There were Centuria, two of them, but without helmets. She'd never seen that before. In all her life in The City, she'd never seen the face of a Centuria.

'I'm Leo and this is Jody. Don't be alarmed, you're safe here.'

Talya sat up straight, alert and ready to fight. She needed more information – the situation did not seem hostile.

'It's okay, Talya, you're among friends. Let me explain what happened. You'll need some time to recover from what we did to you. I'm sorry, there was no other way.'

Talya decided to listen. She didn't think her legs would hold her to make an escape.

'You're in The Climbs,' Leo continued. 'We had to get you away from Fortrillium.'

Talya didn't like the sound of that. She remembered the last things that had happened before she lost consciousness: she was due at a special session the next day. It had all been going wrong.

'How is Lucy? Is she still alive?'

'She's okay, Talya. She's still caught in The Grid, but she's alive. Joe Parsons too, they're both okay.'

Talya was relieved at that. Her last thoughts had been about how she'd let her daughter down by her outburst. She'd given Damien Hunter all he needed to block her. She'd just handed him the rope with which to hang her.

Jody began to speak, on Leo's nod – he'd sensed Talya was going to need lots of reassurance.

'We're sorry we did what we did, Talya, but we had to bring you over from Silk Road undetected. We had to knock you out and take your heartbeat down to zero to pass the scanners.'

'You've been dead for four minutes,' Leo interjected. 'It was the only way we could do it.'

Talya's mind was a confusion of questions and disorientation, and she was unable to comprehend what they were telling her.

'It's all coming to an end, Talya. Damien Hunter would have finished you off tomorrow,' Jody picked up in the silence. 'It was only a matter of time – there's no way you'd have passed through the review process.'

'She's right, you know. Hunter had it in for you.'

Talya recognized the voice, but it was out of place. If they were in The Climbs, why did she hear that voice? She looked towards its source. It was Law Lord Brad Sivil.

'I know I'm the last person you'd expect to see here, Talya, but you have to listen to these people. Whatever you think, we're not the enemy here.'

Talya wasn't so sure about that. She tried to tense her legs again, but they still wouldn't have been able to take her weight. She decided to listen and find out more. She was in their hands for the time being, her body was incapable of resistance.

Jody carried on speaking.

'I know it's a lot to take in, Talya, but this is where The City's resistance movement is based. You're safe here. Your Gen-ID chip is jammed. Fortrillium can't find you now.'

'I'm so sorry about your daughter,' said Law Lord Sivil, 'but really, Talya, you didn't help yourself with Hunter. The man has to be handled.'

'And is that what you were doing, Law Lord Sivil?' Talya snapped, but Sivil seemed different now, he was altogether more conciliatory.

'We all have our roles to play in this, Talya. I played mine well – you had no idea I was part of this.'

'So what is *this*?' she asked, moving her gaze between the three faces in front of her. Her focus was beginning to return. There was activity all around her: medical supplies, food and weaponry.

'This is how Fortrillium will be brought down, Talya,' Jody answered. 'There are many of us in the Centuria who have been planning this for some years now. It was colleagues of ours who brought you through security. President Delman is up to something. We think an important change is about to take place, but we don't know what it is yet.'

'You've brought things to a head,' Sivil picked up. 'Now is the time for us to strike. The attention your daughter's trial has garnered makes this the perfect time to bring down Hunter and Delman.'

'One of our own people was arrested earlier today,' Leo continued. 'They'll torture her and threaten her family. We have to assume they know about us already. We must strike fast.'

'So what am I doing here?'

'Hunter was going to destroy you along with your

daughter. The Law Lords have all been briefed – you would not have made it through tomorrow's review.'

Talya looked at Sivil. She'd thought he was an enemy, but she was unsure now.

'I tipped off Leo and Jody after you left Fortrillium, and they brought you here undercover. Nobody knows you're here. As far as Damien Hunter is concerned, you will not be traceable.'

'But what about Lucy, you fools? He'll use her to get to me. He'll flush me out and I'll have to come forward.'

'Talya, your daughter is dead anyway unless we begin to fight. She was dead the minute she walked into The Grid. That's what Hunter wants.'

Talya knew Leo was right. But Lucy had people working to keep her alive – maybe they didn't know about Wiz, Mitchell and Hannah yet.

'Where do I fit into all this?' she asked. It had dawned on her that they'd just gone through a lot of effort to get her out of Silk Road safely.

'You're a very influential person these days, Talya,' said Sivil. 'People trust you, on Silk Road and in The Climbs.'

Jody and Leo nodded. Talya knew she had influence, they were right about that. It hadn't kept Lucy out of The Grid, however.

'We need a figure to galvanize the rebels, Talya. They need somebody to follow and inspire them when the fight-back begins. That person is you.'

CHAPTER ELEVEN

If Wiz had been able to buy more time for himself, he would have been able to monitor the live message being broadcast from beyond The City's walls. Its recipient was inside The City, seated at a wooden desk in the President's office.

Delman had been perusing The Pact once again. It weighed heavily on his mind. He was sure Hunter was on to him, but so far Mitchell was indicating that nothing was wrong. He didn't trust the little weasel at all, but he was his best source of information.

Teanna Schaelles was troubling him too. She'd been loyal for many years, but she kept pushing and pushing him about the past. If only she'd let it go. He needed to take Teanna with him – she was his security. Her father would do whatever he demanded so long as his daughter was safe. If she didn't return with him, who knew how he'd react?

There was not long to go until Catharsis, only hours until a plan that was a half a century in the making would come together. He'd be out of that wretched place and would be able to put some things right at last. But he had to leave with Teanna. Would she cause trouble when it was time to go?

He read through the final lines of The Pact once again. It would begin at 08:00 hours. He'd make his exit as soon as possible, but not too early. He needed to time it right to keep Hunter off the scent.

Delman tapped an icon on his console and brought up the live feed from The Justice Trial. He'd need The Grid clear by then. If he was going to make a clean exit, it would be virtually impossible to do so undetected during a trial.

He counted up the survivors. There were still too many alive – at that rate the trial would still be going strong. He cursed Damien Hunter for the third time that day. The man was stringing it out, playing the drama on the screens. Well, Delman needed it to be finished, so he'd have to give it a little nudge along.

Josh Delman didn't care what happened to Talya Slater's daughter. His only concern was that Talya should do his bidding. She had been a strategic placement for him in the Law Lords, a way to frustrate Damien Hunter, but if her daughter died in The Grid that was no concern of his.

He would need to speak to his contact beyond the walls. Delman was as certain as he could be that Hunter wasn't on to him. He was sure the line was still safe to use. He sent the encrypted code along the secure line and waited for the answer. He was there, he was reliable, he always responded straight away. What choice did he have, isolated like that?

Delman opened up his voice panel and began to speak.

'I'm coming soon. Is everything ready?'

'I'm ready and waiting for you, sir. It's all as we discussed.'

'I need you to fix something for me. Have you been monitoring the trial?'

'Yes, it's an unusual one. I'm concerned about the new Gridder Janexx2. Her name is Hannah James.'

'What of her?'

'There's something about her gameplay. Most of these Gridders grow up playing console games, but she's different. It's like she took an intensive class. She's not been playing that long, but she behaves like she has. She's studied all of the conventions, legacy and techniques thoroughly. I'm watching her closely, and I've begun to make small interventions.'

'Well, don't worry yourself too much. I want them all dead as soon as it can be achieved without creating any suspicion.'

'What about Fortrillium, sir? If I interfere too much and too early, the Gridders will know something is wrong.'

'Don't worry about it. None of it will matter soon. I want The Grid clear for my exit and I don't want any hitches.'

'Understood, sir. I'll intervene immediately. Do you have any preferences about who should survive until the end?'

'No, kill the lot of them. Do it as and when you can. Just make sure it's empty when I need to exit. There's no room for mess ups – nothing will wait for Catharsis when it begins.'

Delman terminated the connection. As far as he was concerned, there was nothing more to discuss.

At a console in a location beyond The City's walls, Reevil96 shut down his own connection. It was time to intervene in the trial once again. Only this time he wouldn't just be killing the near victor in the final moments of Ascension. This time there would be no Justice Seekers left standing. He was going to have to kill them all if he was to secure his own freedom and save the lives of his family.

Schälen

Lucy had been shocked to find herself isolated once again. She'd only just been reunited with Joe, and now she was on her own once more, with no weapon and Schälen still on the loose.

Perhaps one of the creatures had got him? She doubted it – the man was like a cockroach. He'd probably be one of the last to die. She dared not call out. She was desperate to find her friends again, but she didn't want to draw Schälen's attention. The man was strong, she had no weapon, and her arm was so stiff she wasn't sure what kind of a fight she'd be able to put up.

She cursed Fortrillium and The Grid – their lives were being toyed with for entertainment and dramatic tension. Justice had nothing to do with it. It was just a big game. Moments earlier, she'd been standing next to Joe, armed and able to defend herself. Now she was alone again and defenceless, and if she ran into Schälen, it was not going to be a happy reunion.

Should she stay put and hide until someone friendly passed by? With the creatures still at large, she doubted that was a sensible idea – they'd smell her out. She was vulnerable to attack, from both the monsters and Schälen, and she needed to be able to defend herself. Her friends were in danger too. She couldn't just hide away until it was all over. She'd left Joe and a wounded Ross in the middle of a terrible battle, and for all she knew they could be badly hurt or even dead.

Lucy knew she had to press on in the semi-darkness. There was no hiding now, it was kill or be killed. She took one of the flaming torches from its holder on the wall, so at least she'd have some limited defence if attacked. She resolved to follow the sounds of shouts and roars along the tunnels, hoping to reach the others.

Soon Lucy realized she was being herded. She would follow a sound only to have a tunnel closed off to her by a newly created wall which came crashing down in front of her. She was being guided to a specific location. It felt as if she was circling around in a spiral.

There was nothing she could do to outpace it. Whoever was controlling her movements in the tunnels knew exactly where they wanted her. Lucy followed the path, alert and primed for an attack.

The roars and shouts seemed further away, and she felt as if her next fight was going to be elsewhere, with a very different type of monster. A cold wind rushed up the long tunnel, its icy chill stopping her in her tracks, and extinguishing the torches lining the walls. Her only light was her own small flame, which she'd moved in front of her body for protection.

Footsteps. Slow and deliberate. Something metallic was being scraped along the walls of the labyrinth. She knew what it was before she even saw him.

First his shadow, and then the monster himself stepped into the small area of light cast by the flame of her torch. Schälen was in a state. The bloodied stump where his hand had once been was covered by a section of his overalls which he'd torn off in an effort to stop the blood flow. Even in the darkness it was clear that the bloody, improvised dressing was inadequate for the damage that had been done.

His face was drained of colour and gaunt – he had lost a lot of blood.

Schälen had been running his knife along the wall of the tunnel. He'd seen her before she saw him, and this was a first round of intimidation. However weakened he was, whatever pain he was experiencing – and it must have been a lot – he had only one thing in mind. Lucy was going to pay for what she'd done.

'Nice to see you again, Lucy,' he began, in a measured, sinister voice.

'As you can see, you owe me a hand.'

'It's your own fault, Schälen. You could have worked with us, you know. It didn't have to be this way.'

'It always had to be this way. It's who I am. It's why I'm here.'

Lucy saw the truth in that. It was something in his nature which drove him. The same force was keeping him on his feet, in spite of the massive blood loss, and it would be what compelled him to do what he was going to do next.

Schälen raised the knife to chest level, and Lucy noticed something on his undamaged arm. She moved the torch to get a better look. It was a WristCom. Schälen had a WristCom in the centre of The Grid – how had he managed that?

She barely had time to think. Schälen wasn't there to chat. He lunged at her with the knife and she dropped the torch onto the stone floor. It continued to burn, casting off a limited light, but it was difficult for her to see where Schälen was.

Lucy heard the sound of exits closing all around her. They were being forced into a fight to the death – this was a spectacle for The Grid.

She backed up slowly – she'd lost track of where

Schälen was. Scrutinizing the radius of light further along the tunnel, she watched as a shadow moved along the side of the labyrinth wall. Desperately, she tried to figure out where he'd be in order to cast the dark silhouette, but she was too slow, he was upon her. It was as if he could separate off from his own shadow.

It was Schälen's right hand that had been crushed, but he seemed to be just as powerful when using his left. He struck at Lucy. The blade slashed the flesh on her shoulder and she lurched back, smashing her back against the wall.

He had her trapped, and she was shaken – both of her arms had been wounded now. One was still congealing and raw from his earlier attack, and now her strongest arm was damaged. She could feel her overalls becoming bloody and wet.

She had nothing with which to fight back. He could thrust the knife at her in the darkness and she wouldn't even know where it was coming from. He'd disappeared again, and she saw the shadow once more. He was everywhere, a nest of devils trying to torment her.

The blade cut through her thigh and she screamed out in pain and shock. Her leg buckled. She knew she had to fight. If she fell to the ground she would never be able to defend herself. But Lucy couldn't support her weight, the pain was too much.

As she leaned against the wall, her hand moved to the new wound, hardly daring to feel what damage had been done. She felt a loose flap of skin with the tips of her fingers. It was wet with blood. Her head was spinning.

Then, from the blackness, Schälen appeared again, his booted foot striking the sides of her ankles. Her head thudded against the stone floor as she crashed to the ground, a dead weight. She struggled to steady her thoughts, but she was dazed, in pain and disoriented.

Lucy passed out of consciousness for a few seconds, and when she came round Schälen was kneeling at her side. He was holding up the knife, about to thrust it into her neck. She would have sworn his eyes were red, but she figured she must have been imagining it. Her fight was gone, and there was nothing else she could do. It wouldn't be so bad – he was angry and would finish her fast.

The last thing she was aware of was the flash of the blade as he thrust it towards her windpipe, intent on stealing her final breath.

Sanctuary

There had been no shots fired down the elevator shaft and no flashlights. Every time Wiz eased himself past another closed doorway, he heard activity and commotion, but the Centuria appeared to have discounted the elevators.

None of them worked anymore. It had been years since the elevators in the tower blocks had seen any activity. Some elevator cars had become small apartments for residents of The Climbs desperate for a home. As far as the Centuria were concerned, they didn't exist.

Occasionally, the cables would rot through, or some part of the iron framework containing the elevator mechanism would finally break. Wiz had taken a leap of faith when he'd asked Dillon to jump first. He'd said a silent prayer in the hope the cable could still take their weight. It was a fairly safe bet – the elevator itself was still being suspended between floors below them. When the cables went, the inhabitants of the car would crash to the ground. Wiz knew of an entire family that had been wiped out like this.

'You okay?' he whispered down the shaft to Dillon, unsure of the distance between them.

'I think I'm nearly at the bottom, the cable feels firmer now.'

A few moments later, Dillon confirmed he'd reached the roof of the elevator car. He placed his feet carefully on the surface, relieved to be clear of the precariousness of the cables. There was a creak of old metalwork as his weight put it under a strain that had been absent for many years.

The cable shook as Wiz made his way down, and it wasn't long before he was joined on the car roof. Again, the structure groaned. The car itself moved slightly as it took Wiz's weight.

'We're between floors. They won't find us here unless they figure out we're in the shafts,' said Wiz, catching his breath from the effort of the climb. 'We need to get out of this tower block. When they don't find us on any of the levels, they'll start to ransack the place.'

Dillon looked towards Wiz's voice in the darkness. He couldn't see him at all.

'What do you think happened to Mum?' he asked, scared to hear the answer.

'I don't think they'll kill her,' Wiz replied. There was no point trying to fool Dillon. 'I don't know what they'll do with her, but they won't waste any of us with a quick death, I'm sure.'

Dillon didn't know whether to be reassured or even more terrified. He'd never seen his mother like that before. He'd been so young when Matt died, he'd never known what she was capable of before she was cowed by Fortrillium.

It had shocked Wiz too. She'd been incredible, holding

off the Centuria like that. It had bought them precious seconds in which to make their escape.

'We need to make our way back to Zach's apartment. It should be safe there.'

'You're kidding, aren't you?' said Dillon.

'Where else can we go? We need to set up what I've got left of the tech. They'll keep a watch on your apartment in case you return there, but with Zach gone now, there's no reason for them to monitor it.'

Dillon thought about Zach. He'd been a friend to them all. One of Dillon's earliest memories of The Climbs was how Zach had helped them, before he lost his leg. He'd been like a father to Dillon and Joe.

'How will we get up there without being spotted?'

'Don't know yet,' replied Wiz, 'but I'm sure we'll work it out. We need to get out of here first, though.'

There was a sudden light in the darkness. Wiz's hand had moved to his WristCom. He swung the device methodically from left to right, using the meagre light supply to get a feel for where they were standing. The cables creaked, and a sharp movement caught Wiz off-guard. He hoped it was just the car adjusting to their weight, but he kept his concerns to himself, not wanting to worry Dillon.

'We need to get out of here now. We can't go any lower using the cables.'

Wiz located the emergency trapdoor and gave it a sharp pull.

'Dillon, help me with this!'

They both grabbed the door's handle, tugging and twisting to get it loose. It began to move.

'I'll take it from here,' said Wiz, pushing with every bit of strength he could muster.

It suddenly opened and Wiz was able to lift the hatch.

A terrible smell wafted out of the car, making them both recoil. Wiz positioned his WristCom so he could detect the source of the odour. There was a dead body down there, new enough to stink but old enough to have been there for some time. Some other wretched soul had taken refuge there and hadn't lived to tell the tale.

'We'll have to deal with it,' said Wiz. 'We don't have a choice. Breathe through your mouth, we have to go out this way.'

Wiz went first, helping Dillon down from the hatch. With Wiz's height, it was an easy feat, but for Dillon the drop was a lot higher. As his feet struck the ground, Wiz felt the car sink a little lower. Surely it was just the car taking the cable tension from their added weight? A deep groan from the cable echoed up the elevator shaft. They'd have to move fast – he was not at all sure about the stability of the elevator.

The car had become stuck between levels. Wiz was able to see the exit to whatever level they were on because the inner doors had been prised open by the former occupant. He reached up to try to force open the outer doors, but it was too high even for him to get leverage.

'I'll need to lift you on my shoulders, Dillon. See if you can get your fingers in the gaps and force them open.'

As Wiz took the strain of lifting Dillon, the car sank again. The sound of a reluctant and ageing steel cable sounded up and down the shaft. Gently, Wiz lifted Dillon upwards so he could access what was exposed of the outer elevator doors. Dillon was some time, trying to find an angle where he could gain sufficient traction. After a few minutes, Wiz heard movement.

'I can't get them any wider, but I've managed to make a gap.'

Wiz placed Dillon back on the floor and reached up. Dillon had done well. It was enough of a gap for Wiz to part the doors with his greater strength. He pushed them gently at first – he'd need to check if there were Centuria at that level. All was quiet on the landing. He peered out and could see from the faded paintwork that they were stuck between Levels 18 and 19.

'We're going to have to crawl through that gap. I'll lift you first, then you take my bags and help me up afterwards. If you hear anything, come straight back down and keep quiet. Okay?'

Wiz let Dillon climb back onto his shoulders, and more gingerly this time he took the strain of his weight. There was a slight movement in the elevator, but the cables seemed fine. Wiz stretched up as high as he could to make it easier for Dillon to scramble through the gap in the doors. It was tight. Wiz figured their dead companion must have got trapped that way. Had Wiz attempted to do this alone, he wouldn't have made it. Exiting from the elevator car was a two-person job.

'It's really tight, Wiz, you should have opened it more!' Dillon had managed to place his arms and head between the doors, still precariously balanced on Wiz's shoulders. His weight was supported by the concrete floor of Level 19, but he was struggling to wriggle his shoulders through the narrow gap between the outer doors.

'Lift me a bit more will you?'

Wiz dipped his knees slightly, then thrust upwards to give Dillon the momentum he needed to pull himself out of the car. Wiz knew he'd made a mistake as soon as he'd done it. The elevator sank slightly, there was a creak from the cable above them, then the sound of steel cracking high above.

Dillon cried out – the movement had taken him by surprise, but it was the sound above them that made Wiz's heart leap with fear. From the small gap left by the emergency trap door, Wiz could hear the swishing sound of the heavy elevator cable plunging towards them.

When it struck the roof of the elevator, they would be sent crashing to the ground, eighteen levels below. It would be a few minutes before Wiz died, but in a matter of seconds Dillon was going to be ripped in two, his body severed at the waist by the sudden drop of the falling car.

CHAPTER TWELVE

Endgame

Hannah pounded her fist on the desk in frustration. The other Gridders looked up, and Linwood frowned at her. She was drawing attention to herself, he was warning her not to do that.

She gave a gentle nod in acknowledgment. She felt so helpless – the action was playing out on her console and the big screen in the office, but she had no control over it.

She'd figured out by now where Joe and Lucy were in the scenario. Even though they were represented to her by pixelated characters, their green overalls made identification easy.

Joe was trapped in a corner with one of the creatures. The health indicators of his male companion were poor, and there was no nearby help.

Lucy was in a similar predicament, caught at the end of a tunnel by the serial killer, the other group too far away to help. If only Joe and Lucy had realized how close to each other they were: right at the centre of The Grid, separated by labyrinth walls.

All she could do was to watch the walls come crashing down as her two friends were thwarted at every turn, their chances for escape terminated by some person or player unknown. She'd lost control of the gameplay, she didn't know what to do.

Linwood approached her. There was a high state of excitement among the other Gridders in the room, the action on their screens was exhilarating.

'You're doing it wrong – you're fighting it,' Linwood whispered. 'Every move you make is a counteraction, and whoever is controlling the gameplay is expecting it. Make your move away from the main action. You need to send them on the run.'

Hannah opened a passageway in an area of The Grid which was completely clear of Justice Seekers. Linwood was right, if she went near Joe and Lucy or any of the other players, her mystery opponent blocked her. If she moved away from them, she could create openings in the labyrinth without being blocked. It was counter-intuitive, but it worked.

She became aware of movement at the office door but didn't stop to investigate. It was Centuria, embroiled in a hushed conversation with the Head Gridder. Hannah ignored it.

'We need to open two paths, start wide at the edges of The Grid and map towards the centre. When I say go, open up a route to Joe and Lucy. Keep away from the Justice Seekers, you'll get closed down every time. Make it look as if we're testing new environments in the quiet zones.'

Linwood saw what she was doing and agreed, rushing back to his console. There were large sections of the labyrinth clear, and Hannah began to map an erratic route well away from the main action. They'd both aim for the centre. That way, when she gave the word, they would be able to send Joe and Lucy to the same spot. Not until they'd thrown their hidden opponent off the scent, though.

Hannah sent Linwood the new rendering codes. She was creating a cityscape now, and if she was going to create safe passage out for Lucy and Joe it would need to look as if they were just testing out new environments prior to the final Mode.

Hannah watched as Linwood matched her route, starting out at another clear area of The Grid, mapping out a cityscape pathway which would get Joe and Lucy away from their current peril. Her eyes flickered to the action on the pixelated feed, checking her friends were still alive. She was aware of something going on behind her, more activity from the Centuria who were making their way down to her desk. They were on to her. Her time was nearly up. She typed frantically at her console, watching on her screen as her friends fought bravely to fight off their assailants.

She was going to be too late. She was not going to be able to save Joe and Lucy.

Late Shift

After the drama of the faulty camera, Max had been instructed to work a late shift to make sure there were no more hitches. To lose a crucial camera shot at such an important point of the trial was unacceptable, so for Max that meant a double shift.

He'd opened up a feed of the trial on his console and he busied himself running some routine maintenance checks on the bots. Unusually, there was still one bot left in the centre of The Grid. Due to the rapidly changing nature of the trial, it had been impossible to guide it out safely, so the Gridders had just boxed it in, keeping it out of sight of the main gameplay in a self-contained area away from the Justice Seekers.

It had been a close call when Max sent the commands for the bots to return along the maintenance tunnel and back to his work area. The Gridders had rapidly been opening and closing passageways in the labyrinth and at one stage the Justice Seekers had almost walked straight into them.

A stern memo was issued, and Max found himself on the defensive. He'd negotiated to have the bot contained and the Gridders had obliged, creating a completely enclosed area at the centre. It could wait there until the action died down a bit.

There were more Centuria around than usual. Max was usually left to his own devices; he assumed nerves were frayed by the day's earlier technical difficulties. Still, it was unusual. There was not much about Max's section that was of interest. It was impossible to enter or monitor The Grid – only the bots could go in or out, and all of their operations were remotely controlled.

He rubbed his bandaged hand. It had become a nagging and persistent ache, and he had almost become accustomed to the discomfort. He wondered what Talya Slater was doing. She'd left him well alone after he assisted with the camera operation, even though it had been a mess-up. He hoped she was done with him and his part in the drama would be over.

With all routine jobs completed, Max returned to his console and watched the live stream of The Justice Trial.

He was shocked to see the state of Talya's daughter – he'd watched as the serial killer had taunted and beaten her.

The cameras in The Grid didn't seem to know which action to focus on. The other Justice Seeker in the green overalls was also fighting for his life, hunted by some terrible creature in the tunnels.

Max hesitated and reconsidered his actions. He had no family, so there was nothing for him to lose – Fortrillium could never do to him what they'd done to Talya Slater. But he was just as bad as Fortrillium. He allowed this to go on, and it was he who presided over the carnage.

It was Max Penner who would dispatch the bots to clear up the corpse of Talya's daughter – he would flush away her flesh and bones through the Bio-Shredder. There she'd join the hundreds of other innocent victims who'd perished in The Grid, their decomposing flesh the only memorial to the injustice they'd suffered.

It was there in the silence that Max Penner finally understood his own guilt. It had taken a violent attack by Talya Slater to force him to turn his head and confront the truth. It wasn't Max who sentenced the Justice Seekers or who sent them to their deaths. But it was people just like him who allowed it to continue; by turning away from the horrors and refusing to confront them, he was as guilty as everybody else.

Max's throbbing hand had served as a constant reminder to him of his complicity. It was as if Talya Slater was goading him into action, urging him from afar not to turn the other cheek.

He'd thought he was done with Talya Slater, but he finally understood she'd done far more than just wound him with the carving knife. In confronting him so violently and directly, she'd forced him to see the truth of the situation.

He'd spent his life with his eyes to the ground, never daring to challenge or dissent.

It was time for Max to lift his eyes from the floor and to look bravely ahead. He could do something to help this young girl who was struggling to repel the maniac chasing her with a knife. He could help Talya to save her daughter, and finally do something that might change lives.

Max took a last look at Lucy, then closed down the video feed from The Grid. He opened up a control panel on his screen and keyed in some instructions. In an enclosed area at the centre of The Grid a deactivated bot burst into life. One by one a series of dials illuminated on its side panels. It had received a sequence of remote instructions and was running its tracking software to locate the core of The Grid. When the way finally became clear, this mechanical device was going to perform an operation it had completed many times before, away from the scrutiny of human eyes. It was going to open and close the doorway right at the heart of The Grid.

Slaughtered

Clay had been badly shaken by Grace's death. He'd been distracted momentarily and had been unable to defend her. After separating from Joe, Ross and Lucy, they'd been hunted by the other creature. It had taunted them, charging and roaring, but not attacking. Not for the first time, Clay had felt the hand of intervention in The Grid. He could tell they were being steered and manoeuvered by their distant opponent.

Miron had been formidable in battle. For a man who was in The Grid for arson, his ability with a scythe had saved their skins several times already.

They'd managed to wound and anger the beast, but it didn't seem to be intent on killing them, not at that time at least. It drove them deeper into the tunnels; Clay had completely lost all sense of direction – he didn't know how close he was to Joe's group.

He'd stayed alert – Schälen and Chris were out there somewhere, both were armed though Chris was unlikely to be able to defend himself. Clay was thankful that if one of the beasts was trailing him at least it meant Chris would be out of harm's way. Unless he ran into Schälen, of course.

The creature had continued to force Clay and his group up a particularly long passageway. There were no exits – it just seemed to go on and on. It continued to charge at them, waving its tusks and roaring, then waiting further up the tunnel. Then something seemed to change. The monster tensed, its eyes glowed ferociously in the darkness, and bloody saliva dripped from its deadly fangs. It let out a low growl. Clay couldn't know this was the point at which Reevil96 took over full control of the creature.

It was as if a new monster had just materialized in the labyrinth. Its ferocity and anger were renewed and it prepared to charge once again.

'Get ready!' Clay had warned, and Miron and Grace braced themselves to plunge their weapons into the approaching monster. It let out a bestial roar as it charged directly at them.

At that moment, several doorways opened all around them and Clay's attention was drawn by the sight of Joe in the distance. He began to call out, but the beast had run directly through the middle of the small group, trampling Grace and thrusting Clay and Miron hard against the walls. It flicked Grace's limp body into the air with its tusks, catching her by the neck and tearing her head from her body. It flicked its head in triumph as Grace's head rolled off towards Joe, who was in the middle of his own fight in the adjacent tunnel.

All around Clay and Miron doors opened and exits were closed – it was impossible to chart a path back to Joe. Clay focused on the beast. He was shaken by Grace's bloody death. They'd need to slaughter this monster before they could help Joe.

'Go for its eyes!' Clay shouted to Miron, who was picking up Grace's abandoned weapon. He nodded. The monster turned and began to run at them. Clay looked deep into its eyes. He waited until he could feel the warmth of its stinking breath on his face then leapt at the approaching creature. As he flew over its head, he saw Miron thrust a spear and a scythe deep into the beast's eyes. It roared, thrusting its head upwards and pounding Clay's body against the curved roof of the labyrinth. He raised his arm as high as he could and plunged his weapon deep into its skull. He heard the bones crack as the splash of brains sprayed up over his face. The creature dropped to the ground, dead. Temporarily blinded by the gore, Clay rolled off its back and came to rest at the side of the labyrinth wall.

'You okay?' came Miron's voice.

Clay rubbed his face with his arm, blinking his eyes to remove the remainder of the creature's guts. It was dead. They were seconds away from Joe – they'd lost him again in the confusion of tunnels. But right in front of them, a new exit had emerged. It was like a gateway to a new world – the dark, labyrinthine tunnel merged seamlessly with a roadway in a city landscape. The Grid was changing again, and it was time to run.

20:47 The Core

It was the last thing Hannah did before she was electro-cuffed and violently removed from the Fortrillium building. She opened an exit to two of the Justice Seekers, giving them access to the city landscape and the chance of imme-diate refuge from the claustrophobic tunnels. The path opened before them just as they had slaughtered the beast which had been so intent on killing them.

As she was escorted from the room, the remaining Grid-ders watched her leave, unaware of what she'd done to deserve this unceremonious dismissal. They did not notice her glance in the direction of the man they knew as 97TRaider – it was a momentary look, an assertion that he should not intervene. Instead they continued to work on the plot they'd hatched together. Hannah knew him not by his Gridder name but as Linwood Carley. She hoped it would be his human side that would come to the fore now. Without it, her friends were doomed.

Linwood Carley did not watch his new friend leave the building. Instead, he executed the strategy they'd agreed earlier. He'd lost his brother once, and he knew how hard life could be in The City. He couldn't save his sibling, but he could help his friend Hannah. He'd do what he could.

When Joe Parsons had recovered from the shock of finding Grace Makins' head by his feet, he'd been thrown into a rage of revenge. Seeing that his friend Ross was bloodied and weak, he understood the only way he was going to survive was by slaughtering the creature himself.

The beast had set an ambush, but although it was cruel and merciless, it did not possess the intelligence to outwit Joe. It charged him, just scraping its tusk across his stomach. It tore through his overalls, drawing blood, but not cutting through his skin. Joe had slid under its belly, taking the monster completely unawares.

For a moment, it looked around, wondering where Joe had gone. Then it felt his spear thrusting deep into its heart. It wavered then roared, fiercely trying to locate the predator that had wounded it.

'Ross!' Joe shouted. He'd hurt it badly, but not enough to make the beast perish. Fading fast from his own wounds, Ross rallied to slide his weapon across the floor towards Joe.

It was not quite far enough to reach, and Joe emerged from underneath the creature to grasp for the blade. The beast sensed him immediately and turned, its fangs snapping and ready to crush Joe's bones.

Joe clasped the spear and thrust it into the creature's throat. A gush of putrid air rushed at him, and he rolled swiftly to the side as the vile creation fell dead at his side.

As Joe began to stand up, he was aware of a light emerging way up in the tunnel in front of him. He struggled to adjust his eyes – some new scenario was being created up ahead, but they'd not completed the Mode yet, this was not supposed to be happening.

Far away from The City's walls, Reevil96 was pounding his desk with his fist. He'd been so busy attacking the remaining Justice Seekers that he'd missed being outflanked by Hannah James. She'd created new areas in The Grid, offering a temporary release from the death trap. Although the four creatures of the labyrinth were dead, he would still draw blood on that day.

The killer, Schälen, was about to finish Lucy Slater. His knife was hovering above her head, and he was ready to plunge it deep into her neck, slaughtering her mercilessly as Joe Parsons had just done with the last creature.

Before he could strike, a figure emerged from the darkness, clutching a sharp blade. The Justice Seeker known on the screens as Rampage ran the steel weapon across Schälen's throat: he looked up at his killer and then his limp body slumped on the floor. He'd been finished by the man from the Institute, Chris, who'd found the bravery at the last moment to repay his debt to Lucy.

As Schälen's heart gave its final beat, Chris rushed up to Lucy and a new doorway opened to her side. Before them was a city landscape and a road lined by tower blocks. Further ahead Lucy could see Joe, Clay and Miron. Ross joined them, limping badly, but steadied by Joe.

She grabbed Chris's hand and began to run up to her friends. She stopped suddenly, allowing Chris to walk on, and returned to Schälen's dead body. She'd remembered the WristCom. Lucy wrestled it off his wrist – his flesh was still warm, and she expected him to lunge at her one final time before he went to burn in hell. She held the WristCom firmly in her hand.

Linwood and Hannah had succeeded in bringing them all together again, but the threat of The Grid was not yet over.

Joe rushed up to Lucy, elated to see she was still alive, but anxious to assess the state of the bloody wounds across her body. She moved the WristCom into a pocket in her overalls and embraced him.

Alerted to the sudden crisis, Damien Hunter had demanded the public feed be shut down immediately. The watching crowds in The Climbs and those viewing from the security of their homes on Silk Road were confronted with black screens. Damien Hunter sensed that something was going on; this was Delman making his final play, he was certain. If this was Catharsis at last, he would be reunited with his wife and children soon. He would need to be ready to strike.

As the new tunnels and pathways opened up around them, a bot which had been concealed at the core of The Grid was released from the four walls which had been containing it. It moved purposefully towards a water butt on The City's street and released an activation signal, pre-programmed by a Fortrillium operative called Max Penner. A doorway opened as if from nowhere – the water butt was just a pixelated disguise for the secret entrance which marked the very centre of The Grid. Within the doorway was an elevator, in which was placed a single red button.

Joe saw it first, then Lucy, and they ran towards it. As they did, their bodies were momentarily scanned by some hidden, electronic device. They'd thought in panic it was about to kill them. They were permitted to pass. More pressing though was the weapon fire to the side of them. Clay, Ross, Chris and Miron began to run towards them but were forced to take cover from the bullets.

Reevil96 had taken control of the gameplay once again. He'd positioned deadly snipers in the tower block windows surrounding the square, but he'd been too slow to stop Joe and Lucy. He was desperately trying to re-pixelate the water butt, but the bot had initiated a maintenance mode, and there was nothing he could do to override it.

They stood in the doorway to the elevator, shouting across to Clay.

'Run, take your chance!' he cried to them.

Joe looked at Lucy – they couldn't leave their friends behind at the mercy of The Grid.

There was more weapon fire, and Clay ducked down. It was impossible for any of them to move. Reevil96 had positioned more snipers where they could shoot at Joe and Lucy in the doorway, and they ducked in, frustrated by the helplessness of it all.

Among the bullets and gunfire, a holographic image appeared. They'd seen this before – it usually marked the beginning of a new Mode. But it was not Damien Hunter; this time it was the form of President Delman.

'If you exit The Grid, the consequences for you will be severe,' he began.

'It is forbidden for anyone to leave The Grid by any other route than The Justice Walk. If you take that exit, the penalties will be extreme.'

He looked rattled. Joe had never seen him like that – he always looked so commanding on the screens.

'You have one chance to walk away from this.'

Joe and Lucy looked at each other. To the side of Delman's image, a circle of light appeared. There were five figures in overalls standing in a circle, their faces obscured.

'Take your chance, Joe!' shouted Clay from behind his cover. 'Go now!'

Joe looked at Lucy – they had to see what lay beyond the mysterious exit. Their friends were trapped, and they were on their own. But if President Delman wanted them away from there, they had to be getting near the truth. It was what they'd been fighting for all along. They had to complete their deadly journey. As Joe and Lucy stepped inside the elevator doors, he called out to Clay.

'Take care, Clay. Stay alive!'

Clay waved to him. A spray of bullets was unleashed immediately and he ducked down once again. Hesitating, Lucy took the WristCom from her pocket and threw it as hard as she could towards the other Justice Seekers.

'Take this, Clay,' she shouted over the sound of weapons firing. 'It might help you!'

The last thing Joe saw as the doors closed was the haunted faces of the five figures who were standing beyond the doorway. A group of new Justice Seekers were entering The Grid. Three of the faces were unknown to him, but he was in no doubt about the identity of two of them.

With a bloodied and swollen face, barely able to stand up, he just had time to look into the terrified eyes of his friend Mitchell. Standing next to him, bruised and battered, was his mother.

Unknown to Joe, the man standing next to her was the very person who'd made this exit possible. Max Penner stood fearful but proud, grateful that before he died he'd seen Talya Slater's daughter make her way to safety.

Next to Max Penner, with her back to Joe and Lucy, stood Hannah James, dazed at the speed with which she'd been apprehended by the Centuria and thrown into The Grid.

Forming the final part of the circle was Julia Levett, a former member of the Centuria, who'd been thrown into The Grid for treason, charged with aiding and abetting the conspiracy that was threatening to challenge the rule of Fortrillium.

The very people who'd fought to keep Joe and Lucy alive were now at the mercy of The Grid. Their shackles were released, the bullets fired, and they ran into the ruins of The City to seek protection alongside Clay and the remainder of the Justice Seekers.

As Joe hesitantly pressed the red button in the elevator, he had no idea what hazards awaited the people who'd fought so hard to protect him. Their lives hung in the balance, but Joe and Lucy had no choice. If they were to reveal the secrets of their fathers' deaths they had no other option than to press on.

At that very moment, Joe's brother and his friend were also caught in an elevator. Dillon was seconds from death, while Wiz could only stand there listening to the sound of a heavy steel cable as it hurtled down the shaft towards them.

There were just two people in The City who could watch over them now. One was a Gridder by the name of 97TRaider, who'd become caught up in these events because of a friendship with a new recruit, by the name of Hannah James.

Elsewhere, hidden within the dark shadows of The Climbs, a new leader was about to emerge. She had the influence and power to galvanize the residents of The City, qualities she'd need in abundance in the forthcoming struggle against two enemies who would fight to their last breath to preserve what was theirs.

The elevator reached its destination. It seemed to take forever for the journey downwards to end. Joe looked at Lucy as the doors slid slowly open. Had they stepped into more danger? Would they have been better fighting for their lives with their friends inside The Grid? It was too late now. The decision had been made. The doors opened onto a hi-tech, modern passageway. A group of people was waiting to meet them.

Joe and Lucy stood still. They looked around attempting to determine if they were in peril or not.

A dark-haired man stepped forward, and Joe recognized him immediately. He was older, his hair greyer and he'd grown a beard. He stepped forward and wrapped his strong arms around his son.

'It's good to see you, Joe. What took you so long?'

PREVIEW FROM THE GRID 3

The young doctor studied the viral modelling data on his computer screen, desperately trying to figure out why his attempts at creating a cure had accelerated the death toll. The information didn't make sense. It was supposed to save lives, not take them. They had created two new strains of the disease, and the virus had mutated with a devastating impact. The deployment of a cure had just made the situation worse.

The pandemic had come out of nowhere and was sweeping through urban populations at a rate faster than had ever been seen before. They knew it was airborne, it was infecting just over nine out of ten people and it was spreading like a bushfire across the planet. With two new strains now wreaking fresh havoc, even those who had survived the first wave were in danger once again.

International travel had been stopped too late. They'd grounded the planes several weeks after they should have done. The advisory teams had warned the President at the briefing sessions but he'd ignored them. The Government always assumed the problem would be solved before it became necessary to pull the plug on the airlines.

The protocols were in place, but world governments were always reluctant to shut down cross-border controls. They waited and waited, then acted too late. The plague was going to have to burn itself out, but it would wipe out most of the world's population in the process.

Gripped by a sense of guilt and anxiety, he stayed up into the night when the facility was deserted. They'd all been working ridiculous hours for weeks on end, and the team was beginning to tire. The problem with humans is that they need rest, they have to take breaks, however severe the crisis.

He needed to understand what he'd overlooked. He'd been sure he'd got the cure at last, but it had all gone so wrong. He tested and refined the data then started the process all over again to prove and then re-prove his theory. Every time it pointed to the same thing. There was a reason for the mutations, but so far nobody in his team had seen what was staring them in the face. Even the pooled information-sharing across the world had not spotted this. A single database updated 24/7 with the findings of the best scientific minds across the globe, yet nobody had seen what he'd seen. This was sabotage, and it had taken place at the highest level of government. They'd made him and his team the fall guys. They hadn't even used his cure, they'd gone ahead and substituted the NiVac3 option. It had been hurriedly released and they'd been warned of the consequences. His own solution was more difficult to manufacture at speed, but it would have worked. Now they'd messed up, and they were pointing the finger of blame at him.

The doctor sat in his chair and considered the world

they were about to bequeath to the next generation. Towering walls were being built around major cities on the orders of President James Morgan. Those who'd survived each strain of the plague were being herded into segregated concrete fortresses. The voice of the President was broadcast constantly across all media, issuing instructions calmly and authoritatively. Armed checkpoints were being set up where those who'd survived the plague were to report for sanctuary. The lucky ones who were still alive were barricading themselves in infection-free ghettos, packed with Immunes and survivors. They were all that would be left – humanity was hanging on by a thread.

The Government would struggle to maintain control after this. The existing world order would disappear, too many people had died and it was still far from over. But here was the secret, and nobody had seen it so far. This global catastrophe had been accelerated by the Government. President Morgan had overruled the advice of his advisory panel, rushed through NiVac3, and now the entire world was paying the price.

Significant power resided in this information – he cursed that he hadn't seen it earlier, before it had reached the endgame. It might have been useful then, but there was no longer the infrastructure to deliver a cure globally, not with three deadly strains harvesting so many lives. The plague would have to burn itself out, as it would have done in the Middle Ages.

As a doctor, he was accustomed to healing and curing, but that world of compassion no longer existed. Everything was simplified: you survived or you died. What was happening would divide mankind. Those with the contagion would be left to die and the survivors would cling together, desperate to grasp whatever scraps of humanity they could salvage. He could see it already as the cities were beginning to fall and huge fortresses were being built.

He decided to keep the evidence to himself, removing it from his computer and securely encrypting it on a data card. He had no status now. He'd been shamed and it would take him some time to recover his reputation after such a disaster. The data card would be his free pass – with this knowledge he could wield massive power in the new world that would rise from the ashes of the plague. He had damning evidence against President Morgan and his senior team. Their negligence had caused the Earth to burn. One day, Morgan would be held to account.

He took off his lab coat and placed the data card in the pocket of his trousers. As he was about to walk away, something sentimental in him made him step back. His name badge was still attached to the lab coat. He unpinned it and examined it, recalling the life and career that had once held so much promise for him. That world no longer existed. There was no need for these laboratories anymore, since the plague was unstoppable. They were being hurriedly relocated to a new and secure facility where they would make their final stand against the disease. It was all about the survivors now and the world that would arise from the ashes once the plague had burned itself out. He turned the badge over and put it in his pocket. There was no more need for Doctor Josh Delman. He would have to become something very different in this new world.

Punishment

The Gridders were in a state of high alert. Damien Hunter was paying an unannounced late night visit and the rumour was that he was taking scalps. They'd relaxed too soon, they thought they'd be off the hook once they'd covered up whatever had gone wrong in The Grid. They should have known better. Hunter had been more attentive than usual on this trial, he wasn't going to let it slip. The Head Gridder gave the team a five-minute warning of the visit. They needed to be on their toes.

Hunter had stormed into the room, throwing it into immediate silence. The Gridders stood up when he entered – there was something about the way he burst through the doors that demanded it.

Linwood had taken care to cover his tracks. He knew he was vulnerable because of his collusion with Hannah, but so far they'd left him alone.

There were already extra Centuria in the area, placed there after Hannah's arrest. They seemed particularly alert once Hunter was in the building.

Hunter walked along the rows of desks, saying nothing, just looking at the Gridders. He approached Linwood, he could feel himself sweating. A drop trickled from his temple, down his cheek and onto the floor. Did Hunter see it? He seemed to miss nothing.

Damien Hunter walked up to Linwood, staring him directly in the face. Linwood averted his eyes, not wanting to appear confrontational. He could hear Hunter's breathing. The room was in complete silence.

Without warning, Hunter drew a weapon and placed it to the head of the Gridder who was standing to the side of Linwood. He pulled the trigger. There was a loud bang and the Gridder dropped to the floor. A splat of brain passed Hunter and landed on Linwood's cheek.

A ripple of shock ran around the room, but nobody said anything. They continued to stand in silence, terrified of what he was about to do next.

Hunter barely flinched. His shirt was speckled with the blood of the man he'd just killed. The body was twitching on the floor, it was the only movement in the room. At last he spoke. It was a relief when the silence was finally broken.

'I'm a little bit annoyed about what happened in The Grid earlier. You need to make sure I don't become extremely annoyed. We will now be monitoring all of your consoles continuously for unusual activity. I want these Justice Seekers tormented, but I need to keep a few of them alive, potentially up to twenty-four hours longer.'

Another bead of sweat trickled down Linwood's face. Was everybody else in the room sweating like he was? He daren't turn to look. He thought it must have been obvious to Hunter, but so far no bullet through the head.

'If any of you were working with Janexx2, please step forward now.'

Linwood hadn't been expecting that one. His face reddened, he felt himself burning up. Should he step forward? Would Hunter kill another colleague if he didn't?

'No volunteers? Very well, if you step forward now, your death will be swift. If we find you out later, I can promise it will be very slow and extremely painful. Now, does anybody have something that they want to tell me?'

Linwood hesitated. To step forward would mean instant death. He was no use to Hannah if that happened. Hunter couldn't have known if anybody had been working with Hannah, they'd have been escorted out of the building alongside her if he had. Linwood thought he was safe from detection. Hunter would kill Gridders at random if he wanted to, but there was nothing he could do to prevent that.

Hunter was walking up and down the rows of desks again, looking into the eyes of the Gridders one by one. The tension was electric. Linwood just wanted it to end. He had decided to gamble. Hunter couldn't have known he had been working with Hannah, they'd been careful to cover their tracks. He'd opened up a secure socket before Hunter's announcement so his attempts to track the outside source of interference should avoid the scrutiny of Fortrillium. He'd have to take great care over what help he gave to the Justice Seekers. He was relieved to have placed the MedPacks earlier, before Hunter's visit, he wouldn't have dared do it after the warning was issued.

Linwood chose to stay alive. He was going to help his friend Hannah and the other Justice Seekers. And he was determined to track down whoever was interfering with the trials. He had to find out what was going on. If he was discovered, he'd take his chances. It didn't seem to matter to Hunter if people were guilty or not, everybody's life was balanced on a knife edge anyway.

Hunter stood at the front of the room. There was complete silence again. The body of the dead Gridder had stopped twitching, but there was a large pool of blood around the blasted skull. Hunter spoke again, moving to the side of the Head Gridder who looked as terrified as everybody else in the room.

'I have one more announcement before I leave. We're making an internal re-organization. We're removing a tier of management.'

Linwood looked at the Head Gridder's face. She had guessed what Hunter was referring to. On Damien's final word, she began to run along the aisle between the desks, jumping over the dead body that was obstructing her exit. The Centuria raised their weapons and pointed them directly at her, fingers poised on triggers and ready to end her life.

'Stop!' shouted Hunter, holding up his free hand.

He levelled his weapon, as if he had all the time in the world. The Head Gridder was almost at the office door. Surely they weren't going to let her run? She placed her hand on the ID panel and it turned red.

'Access Denied' came the electronic voice.

Frantically, the Head Gridder placed her hand on the panel again.

'Access Denied.'

She turned to look at Damien Hunter. She knew she was on borrowed time and couldn't believe she was still alive.

Hunter waited until the Head Gridder looked him directly in the eyes, then shot, right in the centre of her forehead. She dropped to the ground. There was an audible gasp this time. The Gridders couldn't contain the tension any longer.

Damien Hunter handed his weapon to a nearby Centuria and began to head for the door, ignoring the shocked faces of the Gridders.

'Consider your department reorganized,' he said, as he stepped over the body of the woman whose life he had just ended.

'Make sure this trial is good, or next time I visit I'll be looking for some new people to fire.'

The last thing he did as he left the room was to turn and point directly at Linwood.

'You're in charge,' he said. 'You have two hours to do better than the dead woman over there.'

Inside The Grid

Throughout The Climbs and Silk Road, the screening of the Justice Trial continued. On the Silk Road side, it was still the main focus of attention. The scenes depicted were dramatic and gripping. Each of the Justice Seekers was being put through their own mental torture, the images of their greatest fears and horrors playing out for everybody to see.

The drones had placed a direct link into the Psyche-Eval implants, allowing thoughts and feelings to be depicted as real-life events. A release of a finely tuned narcotic via the needles that had been shot into the necks of the Justice Seekers ensured there was nothing trivial to see. These were the terrors lurking in the consciousness that sometimes human beings can't articulate.

For Max Penner, it was the fear of being eaten alive by the bots at Fortrillium. He pictured himself being slowly consumed by the serrated metal grinders, his body being pulled through the teeth while he was aware of every moment. The machines spewed his own guts into the disposal pipes, but he was conscious throughout. All Max could feel through the slow horror of the nightmare was that he should have done more to stand up to the injustice and cruelty of Fortrillium.

Mitchell's nightmares were more recent. He was forced to watch as Lucy was peeled, strip by strip, by Schälen. With every scream she made through her agonizing ordeal, she looked him directly in the eyes as if to ask 'What have you done?' He saw Joe tossed on the tusks of the creatures in the Labyrinth, never killed just pierced, scraped, gouged and wounded, but he would not die. As Mitchell was forced to watch, Joe stared at him throughout, asking the same question as Lucy: 'What have you done?' To make matters worse, as the terrifying scenarios continued, Mitchell was joined by Talya, Jena and Dillon. They looked on as Joe and Lucy were tortured, their screams echoing across The Climbs, and all the while their accusatory looks demanding an explanation.

For Jena, the torment was a different one. She saw Joe, Dillon and Matt. They were being hunted by Centuria in The Climbs but they didn't know they were going to be caught. She kept trying to scream at them, to warn them, but she had no voice, they couldn't hear her. She felt a terrible sense of impending doom, but there was nothing she could do. She had to look on in silence as, time and time again, they were captured, tortured and killed.

In The Grid, all that could be seen were Justice Seekers flinching and jumping as if in a fitful sleep, but in their minds the horrors were real, as if they were actually happening. But unlike a dream, the terror did not end, it continued and repeated as the narcotic was slowly released via the needles.

Julia suffered a different type of dream but it was still no relief for her. It fed into her darkest moments and the hideous silences that all humans have to conquer in their own minds.

She saw a baby. It was in a field, crawling along in the grass. There wasn't a lot of grass on Silk Road, and there was none in The Climbs, so to Julia it was a symbol of life and freedom. She'd joined the Centuria because she realized there was no normal life for her – everything in The City turned to dust in the end. As the baby crawled forward, the grass beneath it became black and the clouds above it turned grey. The baby's hands began to burn in the grass, its flesh started to blister and redden, but still it kept crawling. The grass rotted away, the baby began to crawl through filth and rubbish. It became covered with maggots and lice and slowly started to decay. Still the baby kept crawling forward. Its flesh rotted, its eyes dropped out, it began to struggle to move, but still it continued, slowly crawling forward. Eventually, there was not enough flesh to keep the bones together, and the baby decayed into the putrid ground as the dream began again. Julia felt a crushing sense of loss, a sadness for what might have been. It took her breath away.

In spite of his physical strength, Clay too was tormented. What humans can fight off with their hands cannot be so easily subdued in the mind.

Clay's terrors were not of the real world. He conjured up the living dead chasing him through the decaying streets of The Climbs. There were hundreds of them – thousands even – and their grey, rotting hands all reached out for him, trying to pull him down and suffocate him. He ran and fought, he killed the half-dead and repelled them, but still they came. In his dream he had endless energy, he didn't seem to tire, but the battle never ended. He was stuck in a continual fight which had no conclusion. Every moment he felt the adrenalin rush of his struggle for survival, a terrible cocktail of fear and violence.

Every second of their nightmares played out in slow motion in their minds, and on the screens everything could be seen, every detail, every death, every reaction. Heart rates and life-signs data were shown at the bottom of each screen – the hallucinations were placing the Justice Seekers under extreme stress.

For Joe, the dream fed directly into his greatest fears for his family. It captured everything he felt at that moment: the euphoria at seeing his father again after thinking him dead; his love for his mother and extreme frustration with her behaviour – his desire that she'd been stronger when Matt was taken away; his concern for Dillon, who wasn't strong enough, fast enough. It tormented him, slowly, surely, methodically.

In his mind, Joe was running up the stairs of his tower block. He was trying to save his family from some unknown event. He had to get to them as soon as possible. He was desperate to stop for a few seconds to catch his breath, but he knew he was running too slowly, he had to force himself forward. He'd never managed the fifty-two flights of stairs in anything less than eleven minutes before, now he had just ten minutes to reach the apartment and get them out of there.

He'd started out of breath. His lungs wanted to explode with exertion – he willed his legs to move faster, but he could not force any more out of his bruised and battered body.

They'd got so far, so many lives had been lost and they were so close. Now everything was going to be destroyed because of him, because he was unable to summon the resources he needed to rise to this challenge.

They should have suspected the Psych-Evals would be used to manipulate them. Fortrillium had managed to access the deepest secrets of their souls and was now going to use their own fears and weaknesses to destroy them.

Joe counted off the levels one at a time: thirty, thirty-one, thirty-two ... he should have reached thirty-eight by that stage, there was no way he could make it.

Everything in Joe's body screamed at him to stop and give up. He knew he could never make it. Fortrillium had stacked events against him; they'd done this to punish him, he should never have dared to challenge their authority.

As he reached the forty-second floor, the stench of scorched flesh began to permeate the stairwell. The smoke became black and overwhelming as he neared the fiftieth floor, the place where his friend Zach had lived. Another friend who'd lost his life in The Grid.

Joe knew it was over as he reached the floor that had once offered sanctuary to him and his family. He knew what he was going to see when he walked through what was left of the burnt door.

On the floor, with hands and feet bound by wire, were the charred bodies of Jena, Dillon and Matt. They'd punished him for daring to rise against the might of Fortrillium by taking away from him the only thing he had left.

Just as he'd had his family within his grasp and everything he'd always wanted had almost been there for the taking, Fortrillium tore it away from him, dashing his hopes and bludgeoning them on a hard concrete floor.

On the screens, the watching crowds saw Joe's heart rate had rocketed, reaching dangerous levels. Not only did he experience the real physical exhaustion of running up the stairs in his hallucination, he also felt every moment of fear and despair as his family slipped away from him.

Every moment was shared on the screens. The purpose of The Grid was to scare the residents of The City, to make them fearful of speaking out and to ensure they never raised a hand against Fortrillium. However, the effect of seeing these dreams was very different. Throughout Silk Road, and for those still paying attention in The Climbs, it was the humanity of the Justice Seekers that shone through. Here were people just like them, haunted by fears for their loved ones, too terrified to dream of a better life, exhausted by the perpetual struggle to survive. What they were seeing on the screens reflected their own lives, it was their own fears and nightmares they were watching through the eyes of others.

The people being tormented inside The Grid were not evil; they were not the monsters that had been depicted in the promo films and video bursts. They were regular citizens, taking each day at a time, fighting to stay alive and looking out for their loved ones. Their struggle was one and the same. As the scenarios played out on the screens, many on Silk Road turned away, switching off the feeds and preferring instead to spend time with their own families or alone with their thoughts.

Some became aware of more activity on the streets than usual. With the booming of the screen commentaries switched off, the world outside became more visible. There was a tension, a different atmosphere. Some turned their screens back on waiting for an announcement from Fortrillium, an update perhaps. They wondered if there was something going on, events which might interrupt their comfortable lives on Silk Road.

As the scenes played over and over on the screens, they were studied by a lone man sitting in his office. He'd watched the feeds of Joe Parsons and Lucy Slater with interest, but there was nothing much there for him to hold on to. Matt Parsons was still alive, there was a place beyond The Grid – he'd worked that out already. They were all up to speed on that information now.

It was the feeds from President Josh Delman and Teanna Schaelles that were proving far more interesting to him. He'd suppressed them on the main screens minutes after they'd appeared in The Grid. There was no way that he could let the people of The City see the truth about their President.

He'd got a feed patched directly through from the Gridders and he was studying the Psyche-Evals with great interest. He no longer needed to get his hands on the torn-out pages of The Pact. Damien Hunter had access to everything he needed inside the President's head. In ignoring the final words of Reevil96, President Josh Delman had made his first careless move since entering The City. It was going to give his enemy the upper hand. He was about to reveal his own darkest secrets.

The story continues in The Grid 3: Catharsis.

ABOUT THE AUTHOR

Hi, I'm Paul Teague, the author of The Secret Bunker Trilogy and The Grid Trilogy as well as several other psychological thrillers and non-fiction titles.

I'm a former broadcaster and journalist with the BBC, but I have also worked as a primary school teacher, a disc jockey, a shopkeeper, a waiter and a sales rep.

I've loved sci-fi all of my life, starting with the Danny Dunn books and progressing to the huge franchises such as Terminator, Star Trek, Babylon 5, The Hunger Games and The Maze Runner series.

Be first to hear about new books and special offers:
https://paulteague.net